A colorless little man sat fidgeting before an angry Supervisor Jakes.

"Citizen Goodboy, Section G has expended 10 of its most valuable veteran agents attempting to break through the bodyguard of El Primero, the dictator of the planet Doria. All have failed. And now, when I ask the Special Talents Department to send me an assassin who can't fail, they send me . . . you."

"Yes, sir," the little man replied nervously.

Sid Jakes glowered at him. "Could you please tell me *why* they sent you—especially in view of the fact that you've only had one week of training?"

"Yes, sir. You see, sir, I have a special talent—I can . . . uh . . . kill anything."

"How?" Sid Jakes blurted.

"Oh, I think them to death."

SECTION G: UNITED PLANETS

By Mack Reynolds

WILDSIDE PRESS

SECTION G: UNITED PLANETS

Copyright © 1976 by Mack Reynolds

Elements of this novel appeared in *Analog* Magazine under the titles PSI ASSASSIN and FIESTAS BRAVA.

FORWARD

With the advent of the hyperspace drive, man exploded into the galaxy leaving behind an overpopulated Mother Earth. They left like lemmings, streaming out in all directions to find Earth-type planets they could call their own.

No, not like lemmings, for lemmings migrate seemingly without reason, and mankind had its reasons. It had its multitude of reasons, many of them crackpot.

Some sought their own worlds to practice their religion, or lack of it, in the manner they wished, and ranging from Agnostic to Zen. Some fled Earth for socioeconomic reasons, wishing to practice their own politicoeconomic system. They included Anarchists, Syndicalists, Technocrats, Communists of various varieties (including Titoists and Maoists), Socialists of every hue from gentle pink to rosy red. Some of the new worlds, indeed, were settled by romantics who wished to return to feudalism—supposedly a period when knights were bold and ladies most fair. For some, it was race; Blacks to some planets, Orientals to others, Malay to still others. One world was settled by the remnants of the Iturbi forest pygmies of the Congo, and still another by Australian aborigines. Nature lovers, rejecting the automated and computerized civilization of Mother Earth, fled to worlds where they could return to primitive life.

A good many of the pioneering expeditions were inadequately planned and ended in disaster. On various occasions ships crashed on worlds they'd had no intention of visiting. And in various of such cases the pioneers were thrown back into a condition of society they'd had no intention of embracing—like barbarism, or even savagery. Slave societies had sprung up on some worlds, matriarchies on others? theocracies on still others.

It all seemed very chaotic. However, since there was advantage in keeping in touch with each other, United Planets, an extremely loose confederation centered on Mother Earth, was formed and some 3000 of the newly settled worlds joined. Others did not, fearing interference in their internal affairs.

In order to coax the recalcitrants in, Articles One and Two of the United Planets Charter were formulated.

Article One: The United Planets organization shall take no steps to interfere with the internal political, socioeconomic, or religious institutions of its member planets.

Article Two: No member planet of United Planets shall interfere with the internal political, socioeconomic or religious institutions of any other member planet.

For a time, all went well and the race's explosion into the skies continued, colonies often forming new colonies of their own, further out.

But it was then the bomb dropped.

Never before had man run into advanced life forms. But one day a Space Forces Scout found a burnt-out single-seater spacecraft, obviously military in nature. Inside were the charred remains of its pilot, an alien about the size of an Earth rabbit—not that size made any difference. Engineers and scientists, investigating the craft's technology were appalled. It was far in advance of the human race; it was beyond their ability to understand it. In addition, the very fact that the craft was heavily armed and had been destroyed in combat was ample evidence that this alien life form was not necessarily benevolent.

The higher echelons of Earth government went into a tizzy. Sooner or later, man was going to confront this alien intelligence. It behooved him to prepare for the day, advancing his science, his technology, his knowhow, as quickly as possible.

But fully half of the 3000 planets had systems not compatible with rapid technological advance. Some were dominated by far-out religions that wished no changes; some by crackpot socioeconomic systems; some by hermit types, who wanted no contact with other worlds; some by racists who wanted no contact with other races: some by descendants of the Women's Lib movement who wanted no contact with worlds dominated by men.

So it was that Section G, of the Bureau of Investigation, Department of Justice, of the Commissariat of Interplanetary Affairs, was inaugurated.

Section G, supposedly devoted to Interplanetary Security, was actually a cloak and dagger department, devoted to speeding up man's race to the future. Nothing must stand in the way; no government, no religion, no institution. On the face of it, this could not be known to the member planets, or they would have begun dropping out of the confederation like dandruff.

7

I

For once, Supervisor Sid Jakes of Section G, Bureau of Investigation, Department of Justice, Commissariat of Interplanetary Affairs, was flabbergasted. His usual easygoing, happy-go-lucky expression was completely gone.

He said blankly, "You mean Supervisor Li Chang Chu sent you people for this Falange assignment?"

The large one, who had named himself Dorn Horsten, nodded seriously. It seemed difficult for his face to register anything other than stolid sincerity. "That is correct, Citizen Jakes."

The Section G official looked at him in puzzlement. "Horsten . . . Horsten . . . Dorn Horsten. You're not Doctor Horsten, the algae specialist?"

"That is correct."

"But . . . but what are you doing in my office? In Section G? Li Chang was shaping up a small troupe for me to send to a far-out planet that's been giving us a hard time."

Horsten nodded. "I understand the size of your organization precludes you knowing all your agents, Supervisor Jakes. I was recruited by Ronny Bronston, after he had saved my life under somewhat remarkable circumstances. Although I embrace the purpose of Section G as

9

ardently as any other agent, thus far I have been utilized on only two assignments."

Sid Jakes shook his head and turned to the middle-aged couple seated sedately before his desk. The woman was small and demure, somewhat mousy; the man was on the plumpish side. He had a feeling they were servants —a couple for long years in service, he perhaps a butler, she a maid, or cook.

Sid Jakes said, trying to shake his tone of despair, "And you two are also Section G agents?"

"We three," the man said.

Sid Jakes stared at the little girl in her pink go-to-party dress, a blue ribbon in her neatly combed blonde hair to match her baby-blue eyes. She was, Sid figured, going to be a beauty when she grew, but what the hell did that have to do with this situation?

He blurted, "How in the world did you get past the Octagon guards with that child?"

The child tinkled a laugh.

The woman said, "Helen is . . . is it twenty-five?"

"Twenty-six," Helen said. She made a childish face at Sid Jakes, who blinked.

The woman, who had been introduced as Martha Lorans, said, "Helen isn't really our daughter, of course. It's camouflage. In putting the team together, Li Chang thought it would do nicely as protective coloring."

"Especially," Helen said, "since I'm so conspicuous otherwise."

"But . . . then you're a midget," Sid Jakes blurted.

"Not exactly," the seeming child said, an element of irritation in her voice. "There's a situation on our planet that thus far our research people haven't solved. For that matter, we are not so sure we wish to solve it. What is the basis of the belief that people should strive to be taller? Why was the Viking the ideal, rather than the Japanese?"

"For one thing," Doctor Dorn Horsten said, deadpanned, "the Viking could clobber the Japanese."

She looked over at him and snorted. "Not always, you big lummox. It was the Japanese who perfected judo and karate, remember. But even if it was true that in the old days of swords and spears the large man dominated the small, we don't use such weapons now."

"What started all this jetsam?" Sid Jakes said. The interview had a feeling of unreality so far as he was concerned. He had more than an averagely serious situation on his hands, and had requested a team of trained Section G operatives. His colleague, Supervisor Li Chang Chu, had sent him what would appear to be an average middle-aged family—man, woman and eight-year-old child, and a staid, though admittedly king-sized, scientist of interplanetary reputation.

Helen said, "I was just telling you that on my home planet, of Lilliput, we are small in stature, as averages go, and we are also long-lived and mature rather slowly, in so far as appearance is concerned. In my case, of course, we are relying upon children's clothes, a child's hairdo, and even a certain amount of cosmetic to help put over the effect desired."

"The effect desired?" Sid Jakes said blankly. "What in the name of the Holy Ultimate did Li Chang think the effect desired was? I need a troupe of agents, tough agents, to lick the situation on Falange."

"How tough?" Helen said sweetly. She had allowed the childish lisp to return to her voice.

Sid Jakes glared at her. "Tougher than any seeming

11

eight-year-old kid could handle." he snapped. "Listen, they're onto Section G on this planet Falange. We've lost three agents there in the past year and a half. In each case they were unmasked and brought to trial on trumped-up charges. One was accused of murder, one of subversion and the other disrespect of the Caudillo; all capital offenses. Their *Policia Secreta* is one of the most efficient in the some 3000 worlds of United Planets. They ought to be, they've had enough practice. And now they're just sitting there, waiting for the next batch of Section G operatives to show up."

Sid Jakes came to his feet suddenly, paced around the desk and up and down the floor, in sheer disgust. "It's going to be a neat trick to even land there, not to speak of overthrowing the crackpot government."

"Overthrowing the government?" Pierre Lorans said interestedly. "Li Chang didn't tell us what the assignment involved."

The Section G supervisor turned on him. "I suppose that if you've made agent in this bureau you must have something on the ball. What did you do before you were recruited?"

"I was, and am, a chef," Lorans said.

"A chef!" Sid Jakes rolled his eyes upward in search of divine guidance. Then he looked at the woman. "And you?"

"I'm a housewife."

"A housewife. Holy Jumping Zen. Except for the training I *assume* Li Chang put you through before making you a full agent, did you have any earlier background that would. . . ."

She shook her head. "No. Not exactly."

He rounded the desk again and plumped himself

down in his swivel chair. He closed his eyes and said, "I give up. I surrender. Three of our best agents down the drain and to replace them I get a double-domed scientist, a pint-sized girl in baby get-up, a chef and a housewife."

Doctor Dorn Horsten lumbered to his feet. He was a big man, at least six foot six and must have gone some two hundred and forty pounds. However, his conservative dress, his pince-nez glasses and his scholarly facial expression, tended to offset his size.

He said gently, "Helen, I suppose we should make some effort to indicate why Li Chang Chu chose us for this assignment."

The little girl looked up at him in wide-eyed innocence. "Allez-Oop!" she tinkled suddenly.

In a blur of motion, the hulking scientist reached down and grabbed her by the feet, swung her mightily, in a giant circle, launched her brutally at the far wall, head first.

Sid Jakes' eyes bugged. He came half way to his feet, froze momentarily, and sank back again.

Helen turned in the air, her small arms tucked around her knees, hit the wall, feet first, bounced upward, hit the ceiling, feet first, richocheted off to a set of steel files, bounced onto the desk of the Section G supervisor, seemed to go up into the air and spin around three times. She wound up sitting on his shoulder, his paperknife in her tiny, chubby hand. The point of the paperknife was behind his right ear.

Doctor Dorn Horsten nonchalantly picked up Sid Jakes' ultra-large steel desk, tucked it under his left arm and walked over to the wall where he leaned, on his right hand, still holding the desk.

13

Horsten said mildly, "The widely held prejudice that double-domes—I believe that was your term—don't have muscles fails to stand up on my home world of Brobdingnag, Supervisor Jakes. You see, we have a 1.4 G planet. On top of that, the original colonists were, ah, nature boys, I believe is the usual term of contempt. At any rate, in the same manner that Helen's world possibly has the smallest average citizen in United Planets, surely Brobdingnag has the strongest."

Sid Jakes was still in a state of shock. He stared at the desk under Horsten's arm, and blurted, "You can't pick that up."

Dorn Horsten let his eyebrows rise.

"It must weigh a ton!" Jakes protested.

"I doubt it," Horsten said easily. "It doesn't really have the heft."

Helen, with a skip and jump, bounced from her superior's shoulder to the floor and in a graceful, flowing motion, back into the chair she had originally occupied. In childish modesty she arranged her skirts over her knees.

The overgrown doctor returned the desk to its place, with apologetic air. "It speeds things up, sometimes, to be a bit melodramatic," he said.

Sid Jakes closed his eyes and rubbed them with his right hand. He opened them again and looked accusingly at Mr. and Mrs. Pierre Lorans.

Pierre Lorans shifted in his chair slightly, cleared his throat and said, as though it was the most reasonable thing in the world, "I throw things."

"I'll bet you do," Jakes muttered. "What do you mean, you throw things? What, and, above all, why?"

"Well, it's always been a hobby. Ever since childhood

14

I've gotten a kick out of throwing things." He came to his feet and approached the Section G official's desk. "For instance," he said and picked up the paperknife.

The office of Sid Jakes was done in a British Victorian revival motif. At the far end of the more than averagely large room was an antique calendar.

"For instance," Lorans repeated and suddenly flicked the paperknife. "It is June 23rd, old calendar, isn't it?"

Jakes' eyes went to the calendar. "Hey," he said. That's a collector's item!"

The professional chef took up an ancient pen, a decorative antique on the supervisor's desk. That flicked suddenly, too, and also buried itself in the tiny square devoted to June 23rd.

He turned back to his superior. "I throw just about anything. Knives, spears, hatchets, meat cleavers. . . ."

Jakes shuddered.

". . . ball bearings——"

"Ball bearings?" Jakes said.

"Ummm," the plump man fished into his jerkin pocket and came forth with a shiny steel marble. "You'd be surprised what you can do with a ball bearing. See the right eye in that portrait down there?"

"Oh no you don't. . . ." Jakes said, much too late.

The ball bearing, instead of bouncing off, penetrated the eye completely and evidently imbedded itself in the wall beyond.

". . . baseballs," Loran was saying, "boomerangs, shovels, crowbars, wrenches. . . ."

"Shovels!" Jakes said. "All right, all right. Sit down. Don't throw anything else. I accept your word." He bent his eyes on Mrs. Lorans. "Do you throw things too, or is it only a one-member-of-the-family vice?"

15

"Oh no," she said primly. "Pierre and I met at the Special Talents class of Supervisor Li Chang——"

"Is *that* where she dug you all up?" he muttered. "I'm going to have to find the time to look into that pet project of Li Chang's."

"We attended at the same time. I'd never seen anyone throw things before. Not like Pierre does. He's an artist. You should see him throw a fork."

Sid Jakes looked pained and muttered something about inviting him to dinner, but then he said, aloud, "And your, ah, Special Talent?"

"Well," she came to her feet and approached the antique book shelves, and selected a volume of the *Encyclopedia Britannica.*

"Holy Jumping Zen," Jakes snapped. "Easy with that. It's worth its weight in platinum. Don't throw it!"

"I wasn't going to throw it," she said. She put it down on the desk, opened it at random, spent possibly one flat second scanning the page, then pushed the book in front of Jakes and returned to her chair.

He stared at her.

Her eyes went vague and she began to recite. *". . . which is shown a lion holding a sword. The whole has a border of yellow. This flag was first hoisted on the morning of February 4, 1948 and became. . . ."*

She droned on and on.

Sid Jakes scowled, looked from one of the four to the other, and finally looked down at the book. He blinked.

Mrs. Pierre Lorans was reciting, word for word, the encyclopedia's article on flags. Word for word, without a single mistake.

"All right," he interrupted finally. He looked at her accusingly. "You could do the whole page?"

16

"Yes."

"You could do the whole Encyclopedia?" he said unbelievingly.

"If I scanned each page."

"Holy Ultimate, why don't you rent yourself out as a computer memory bank?"

"I have held somewhat equivalent positions," she said, folding her hands and lapsing back into her housewife role.

Sid Jakes sat there for a long moment, looking at them. Finally he said, "Forgive me, but frankly you four are the most unlikely set of freaks I've ever had in my office."

Doctor Dorn Horsten said stolidly, "Actually, we are not as far-out as all that. It is just that you are seeing us all together. In truth, man has always been a freak among animals. And right here on Earth, in the old days, there were men who trained themselves to the point where they could pick up 4000 pounds, two tons. There were others who could run down a wild horse and capture it. There were gymnasts that could put a monkey to shame. There were others with eidetic memories, such as Lord MacCauley, still others with freak brains who could do fantastic mathematical problems in their heads. I will not even mention various well-authenticated psi phenomenon, ranging from levitation to clairvoyance."

Sid Jakes pushed his hand back through his hair and said, "All right. But the thing is, what'd Li Chang have in mind when she sent you here?"

Helen looked at him mockingly, her childish eyes bright. "But you've already mentioned the reason. How did you put it? The *Policia Secreta* of the planet Falange is onto Section G and they're just sitting there waiting for the next batch of agents to show up."

He contemplated her.

She shrugged tiny shoulders. "Did you expect your next troupe to be able to land with Model H guns and all the gadgets of the Department of Dirty Tricks? They'd be detected before the spaceship ever sat down."

Some of Sid Jakes's natural exuberance returned to him. "Holy Ultimate," he muttered. "At least they're going to have some surprises coming. But what's the excuse for your going to Falange? They don't welcome strangers. Tourists are not allowed. They're one of the most backward worlds in United Planets and want to keep it that way."

Horsten said, "All worlds settled by man owe their existence to the chlorophyll-containing plants. All of them have problems involving algae. Supervisor Jakes, I do not know of a world with any science whatsoever that would not welcome a visit by Dorn Horsten. Excuse me, I speak in all modesty. With but the slightest drop of a hint to a colleague on Falange and I would be overwhelmed with invitations."

"Hmmm," Sid Jakes said. "I suppose you're right." He looked at Pierre Lorans.

The plump man who liked to throw things, puffed out his cheeks. A certain Gallic quality seemed to come over him. He said pompously, "I am a Nouveau Cordon Bleu chef. One of my specialties is the dishes of the Iberian peninsula. I assure you, my *paella* is unsurpassed. At this time, however, many of the dishes once famed in Spain can now be found only on the planet Falange where they were taken long ago when that world was colonized. Supervisor Jakes, there are few, if any, worlds where a Cordon Bleu chef would be unwelcome. Haute cuisine is one of the gentler arts. I will arrive with the announced intention of studying the dishes of Falange, in addition to giving of my knowledge and skill to chefs residing there. I will, of course, be accompanied by my somewhat, ah, forgive me Martha, colorless wife, and my pretty little girl. What could be more innocent?"

Sid Jakes took them all in again, one by one. He grinned. "It'll be a neat trick," he said. Then, "Let me brief you on the situation." He squirmed nervously in his chair, more his old self at last. He said, "You know, most people are in favor of progress. Of course, it's an elastic term. For instance, some centuries ago early nuclear physicists devised a method of splitting the atom. Their discoveries were turned over to the military which utilized them to blow up a couple of cities. It all came under the head of progress. Earlier still, missionaries landed on the islands of the South Pacific. Within a century, the populations had been decimated. However, they had been baptized before succumbing to tuberculosis, syphilis and measels so the missionaries considered it progress."

Martha Lorans laughed, displaying a desirable side of her that had thus far been hidden. She was almost attractive when she laughed.

Sid Jakes said, "However, some people are not in favor of progress in *any* form. And the ruling elite of Falange are among them. Have any of you ever heard of the Spanish Civil War?"

The three Lorans shook their heads but Doctor Horssten scowled seriously and said, "Slightly. Nineteenth or twentieth century, old calendar, wasn't it?"

Jakes said, "It was a strange war. Supposedly a civil war, it was actually a preliminary conflict preceding a global one. Spain was used as a proving ground for

19

weapons and troops; tens of thousands of Europeans, Asiatics and Americans swarmed there to participate. It was a brutal war and it devastated Spain. When the smoke cleared, the forces of the Fuhrer and Il Duce had enabled the more reactionary elements to come to power under their own dictator, El Caudillo.

"However, no problem is ever settled until it is settled right, and the elements that had achieved power under the Caudillo were not those needed for the country to develop. The government and the socioeconomic system were anachronisms and it began to show. While the rest of Europe snowballed into the Second Industrial Revolution, Spain remained stationary. Soon, the more intelligent and trained elements in the country realized the situation and began to take what action they could. The very things that El Caudillo had won on the battlefields, he lost in the day-by-day developments of civilian life. Uneducated peasants cannot be trusted to operate machinery—schools had to go up. Underpaid workers are inefficient—pay began to go up. Tourists don't come to countries where there are terrifying secret police everywhere—the *Guardia Civil* was cut down numerically and no longer paraded the roads and bridges openly armed with submachine guns. Slowly, the Caudillo's victory was eroding away.

"Most of the Spanish, of course, were profiting by this and most were pleased. Spain eventually boomed to the point where it entered Common Europe. However, there was a hard core who objected. They lived in the past and wanted to stay there. They had won their reactionary war behind the Caudillo and demanded that what they had won be forever preserved. When this became impossible, in Europe, they became one of the first groups to colonize another world—Falange."

Little Helen was frowning. "I can see these stick-in-the-muds wanting to maintain their old privileges, their positions of power. I can see them deciding to migrate to a new planet where they could, uh, go to hell in their own way. But I can't imagine them getting enough peasants, servants and so forth to go with them. And a ruling elite is no longer a ruling elite, unless it has somebody to rule."

Sid Jakes chuckled. "You're wrong there, my dear. In any given social system, the majority of the ruled like to be ruled in the manner in which they are being ruled. Otherwise, they'd do something about it. Under slavery, the majority liked being slaves, or they would have taken measures to end the situation. Under feudalism, the serfs, the artisans in the towns and the middle class merchants all liked being ruled by the aristocracy. When they stopped liking it they stormed the palaces and some clever chap invented the guillotine to speed matters up."

Helen made a face. "I suppose you're right," she said, "but you'd have one hell of a time making a slave or serf out of me."

Jakes chuckled again. He was beginning to like this pint-sized operative. "I am sure you would either become free or die in the attempt, and, of course, a dead slave is not a slave. At any rate, our malcontents were able to recruit all the elements they needed for their new colony. Several thousand strong, they migrated. Their new society was dedicated to the past and the prevention of change. And there it is today."

"And that's where we come in," Doctor Horsten said. "But why?"

21

SECTION G: UNITED PLANETS

Sid Jakes looked at him. "Surely you know that. You're a Section G agent."

Pierre Lorans said, "Obviously, we know the reason for the existence of this cloak and dagger department. It is to forward the progress of the worlds settled by man so that we will be as strong as possible, as a life form, when our inevitable confrontation with the intelligent aliens beyond takes place. But why the need to overthrow the government of Falange?"

The Section G supervisor nodded. "Whether they want to be forwarded or not, and most of them don't, our task is to push our member planets into progress. Nothing is clung to so assiduously as socioeconomic systems, and nothing can become so detrimental to progress. The immediate factor that motivates us is that the most highly industrialized planets, for example Avalon and Catalina, are somewhat desperately in need of various rare metals that are present in ample supply on Falange. Mining methods are so primitive there that unless she is more highly industrialized and welcomes in engineers from more advanced worlds, these minerals will never be exploited."

Doctor Horsten had taken his pince-nez glasses from his nose and was polishing them. "Very well, our task will be to overthrow this restrictive government and establish a new regime more conducive to progress."

Sid Jakes looked at the four of them doubtfully. It was, of course, partly their clothing and deliberate effort to look harmless. But for the moment a more unlikely group of revolutionists could hardly be imagined.

Pierre Lorans said, "Just what is their present governmental form?"

22

"An absolute dictator," Jakes said. "The Caudillo, who rules for life."

Lorans said, "But the regime has been in power for centuries. When the Caudillo dies, how does a new one come in?"

Jakes looked around at them. "The best matador is appointed."

The four stared at him.

"The *what?*" Helen demanded.

"The best bullfighter."

II

Irene Kasansky looked up when Derek Lamb entered the reception room of the sanctum sanctorum of Commissioner Ross Metaxa. She knew every agent in Section G—which was probably more than the commissioner himself or his chief assistant, Sid Jakes, could boast. She said, "Hello, Derek. Watch it today. The jetsam is flying."

He grinned at her. "As always," he said. "Can I get in to see the Chief?"

"Probably. Just a minute." Irene efficiently flicked switches, and said some things into a screen. She listened a moment, then snarled, "I quit," flicked another switch and said to Derek Lamb, "You can go on in."

He hesitated for a moment and said, "Is there anything on Ronny Bronston?"

A shade came to her perky face. It was well known that Irene Karansky had a crush on Supervisor Ronny Bronston. She said, "No. No word. He's disappeared." She hesitated before continuing, "Presumed dead, like the others."

24

"I see," Derek said. He added, "On my last assignment he saved my life."

She looked after him as he turned to enter the inner offices. Derek was one of the best ones, she knew. He was a tallish, gangling type, the last you'd expect to be an operative in Section G. In spite of the fact that he was about thirty, his face had an open, boyish quality, kept from handsomeness by slightly buck teeth. His grins were frequent and people were apt to take to him. But it was also known that Derek Lamb was as dedicated as they came. Ross Metaxa used him on the hard assignments, the ones most Section G agents disliked.

Derek went through the door behind her desk, turned to the left for a few steps and came to a door inconspicuously lettered *Ross Metaxa, Commissioner, Section G.* He knocked and it opened.

Ross Metaxa was no beauty. In his late middle years, he had been the head of Section G for more than two decades, and it showed. It had soured his face, thickened his waist—since he seldom left his desk—and brought a weary cynicism to his eyes. He invariably looked as though he had either drunk too much the night before, or slept too little.

He looked up from the papers he had been staring at glumly and said, "Sit down, Lamb. Let me see, what in the hell was it you were on?"

Derek sat, then replied, "Stalin."

"Stalin, Stalin . . . oh, yes." He reached into a desk drawer and came up with a brown bottle and two shot glasses. He poured for them both, and said, "You know why I picked you for this Stalin project?"

Derek took up his glass. "No."

"Because you're one of the few agents I've got who'll

25

drink this Denebian Eight tequila. Only a planet settled by Mexicans could turn out enamel remover like this."

Derek knocked back his shot of the impossibily strong spirits without apparent effect. "What's that got to do with Stalin?" he asked.

Metaxa said, "One of the few things I know about Stalin is that they drink there. And I mean *drink.*" He tossed his own tequila back over his tonsils. "Another one?" he asked.

"Why not?"

The commissioner poured and said, "All right. What did you find out about Stalin?"

"There's damn little in the data banks."

"I know. Brief me."

Derek crossed his legs and rubbed his slightly protruding teeth with the forefinger of his right hand. He said, slowly, "It's one of the far-out ones. Why they ever joined United Planets, I don't know."

"Because of Articles One and Two. It protects them from outside interference. They've got a phobia about having their internal affairs messed in."

"That they have. Theoretically, they allow no visitors whatsoever, and carry on practically no interspace commerce. They have an artificial satellite circling the planet. Any communication with other worlds goes on through it. No visitor lands, not even a United Planets representative, not to speak of a Section G agent."

"What's the background?" Metaxa growled.

At that moment, one of his desk communicator screens lit up. He growled into it, "Don't bother me with such trivia, turn it over to Sid Jakes." And then, "All right try to transfer. But you'll find no other department will have

26

you. Everybody in the Octagon knows your nasty temperment." He flicked off the screen and said to Derek, "I don't know why I don't fire her."

Derek said mildly, "Because Irene knows more about the workings of this department than you do."

Metaxa scowled at him. "Where in the hell were we?"

"The background. This is one of the really far-out planets, Chief. I don't know how much you know about Earth history, but when the communists took over in Russia in the 20th Century, they were orthodox reds, as they called them then. But things evolved. After a time the Old Bolsheviks were old hat. As the country industrialized, these bureaucrats became an anachronism. With computers, automation, and so forth, they became more and more in the way. The new Russians needed political bureaucrats like a few extra holes in the head. So they tossed most of them out. These believers in the old, let's say pure, communism, took off for a planet of their own. They called it Stalin. And there it is, still grinding on with the socioeconomic system that prevailed in Russia in the 1930s, Old Calendar."

"How's their economy?"

"We don't know much about it, in view of their not allowing foreign visitors. But probably backward, comparatively. The bureaucracy is probably afraid that if they allow innovations it might lead to further innovations like changes in who runs the country."

Metaxa said thoughtfully, eyeing his bottle of Denebian tequila, but evidently finding the strength to refrain, "They sound as though they'd give damn little support when we confront the aliens."

"Yes."

27

"We need more information. We need a preliminary survey. Then possibly we'll have to send in a team to throw these communist bureaucrats out."

"Yes."

Metaxa said, "But how can we get a man in?"

Derek told him.

III

Supervisor Li Chang Chu said, "But Sid, are you sure? I have never approved of personal assassination."

Sidney Jakes was less than his usual exuberant self. His face was as unhappy as his colleague's. He said, "There's no alternative, Li Chang. This is the third troupe we've had swallowed up in the maw of El Primero's goonies. He's built a police state of a power unknown since Adolf the Aryan's under Himmler. We've got to get rid of him."

She was less than convinced. "Why the immediacy? Suppose it came out? The reputation of Section G is already so high that if something like this—— -"

Sid Jakes was making negative motions with a forefinger to interrupt her. "That's the point," he said. "This Michael Ortega, El Primero of the planet Doria, has our number and he's using it to club us over the head. Commissioner Metaxa made a mistake when he revealed the true nature of United Planets to so many chiefs of state. Too many were allowed to know that the basic *raison d'etre* of our organization is to push scientific, industrial, and technological progress, no matter what institutions might stand in the way. Some, evidently, leaked it."

SECTION G: UNITED PLANETS

The diminutive Chinese woman—more a girl, in appearance—shifted her slight, cheongsam-clad figure in her chair. "But what is he doing?"

Sid Jakes grunted disgust. "Seemingly, not much. He invokes Article One of the Charter, and he threatens, if we persist in opposing his policies, to pull out of United Planets, and, further, to reveal to the total membership of the confederation the fact that Section G has been subverting the institutions of the more backward worlds. Which, of course, we have been doing in our attempts to get them moving."

Li Chang Chu said, "I'm not up on Doria. What are the particular institutions blocking progress there?"

"A personal dictatorship interested in maintaining the status quo at any price."

Li Chang said, in protest, "But Sid, we have many kinds of tyrannies in United Planets: religious hierarchies, industrial feudalism, matriarchies, patriarchies——"

Sid Jakes was waggling his finger at her again. "Not like this. He's comparable to Russia's Stalin, to the Dominican Republic's Trujillo, back in the Twentieth Century."

A frown of Li Chang's face was a gentle thing. She said, "I've heard of Stalin, of course."

"Trujillo. Rafael Trujillo," Sid Jakes said impatiently. "Trained by the United States Marines in the days when, at the drop of a sombrero, the marines landed in any Latin American country that didn't toe the United States line. Back in the 1920s when the marines were making the world safe for those who had them."

He snorted amusement, the usual Sid Jakes coming out for a moment. "With American backing, he seized

30

power in 1930 and held onto it until he was shot in 1961. During those thirty years he ruled absolutely for himself, his family, and a small circle of associates. He milked his country dry. Finally, even the American elements that had originally supported him got fed up. But he lasted more than a generation, Li Chang. We can't afford to have Ortega do the same."

Li Chang Chu looked unhappily about the Octagon office in which they sat. She said, at last, "But assassination. My experience has been that it seldom accomplishes the desired result. Take the Grand Duke Ferdinand. The South Slavonian patriots who shot him, hardly expected his death to precipitate the First World War. Take Philip of Macedon, an extremely capable organizer, cut down in his capital. The result? Alexander, his son, evidently a god in physical appearance but no great brain, rampaged through the civilized world with Philip's army, butchering millions to build his empire. And what happened to it after his drunken death? It fell apart and for generations his generals and their sons, and their sons, fought it out, destroying Greece and the Near East to the point where the stolid Romans were able to take over."

"Two examples," Sid Jakes grimaced.

Li Chang said softly, "The most famous lynching of all time didn't silence the teachings of the Rebel."

Sid Jakes looked at her in speculation. His own voice was impatient. "Are you so sure? I assume you refer to the troubles in ancient Jerusalem. True enough, His name went on, but did His teachings? Assuming He had original teachings? It has been debated."

Li Chang frowned. "The Sermon on the Mount went on, even though He died."

"There is nothing original in that sermon. It is all to

31

be found in the writings of the latter prophets in the Old Testament. I was referring to original teachings. If He had any, they were soon forgotten, or deliberately suppressed by those who called themselves followers, but who had their own axes to grind."

"But . . . the Golden Rule."

"Ye gods, you babe in the woods," Jakes snorted. "The Golden Rule hardly originated with Joshua of Nazareth. There's hardly been a religion, holy man or even a philosopher, who hasn't stated that bit of truth, down through the ages."

He turned grimly serious. "Enough of this arguing, Li Chang. El Primero must go. We can't allow him to hang on for generations. Doria is crucial in the economic development of United Planets. We can't have this ruling hierarchy, headed by Ortega, continue to drag their heels. We need an assassin. You say we have one in this Special Talents group of yours?"

"Yes, we have one," Li Chang Chu said softly. She came to her feet, preparatory to leaving.

Sid Jakes said, "Send him in. We've lost too many good operatives on Doria. El Primero has got to go."

She hesitated before turning to leave. "Any word about Ronny?"

Again his face was empty. "No, We haven't been able to raise Ronny Bronston, or any of his troupe. We can only assume the secret police got to him, Li Chang."

He knew goddamned well she was in love with Ronny Bronston. Which made him envious, but, on the other hand, he liked Ronny, too. The guy was his best troubleshooter-hatchetman.

SECTION G: UNITED PLANETS

Her words were barely audible. "I see. I'll send Sam in, Supervisor Jakes."

"Sam?"

"The assassin you wanted."

IV

It had been decided that there was no particular reason for them to avoid each other in the Spaceship *Golden Hind*. The most natural thing for the noted Doctor Dorn Horsten, who was traveling alone, would be to strike up a companionship with Chef Pierre Lorans and his wife Martha since they were all headed for a common destination, the Planet Falange and its capital city Nuevo Madrid.

Thus, early in the journey the Doctor introduced himself and soon became the constant companion of the chef who specialized in Iberian dishes. They spent considerable time playing battlechess while Mrs. Lorans read through the ship's tapes, and little Helen played with the scant supply of toys she had been allowed to bring along.

The child was a good-natured, cheerful tyke, the other passengers decided, usually with a slight smile on her face, as though she was amused by some inner thoughts. She was obviously too young to have much understanding of the adult world, and businessmen or diplomats paid no attention to her if she sat at their feet during a discussion.

On the third day out, Earth time, Helen came to where

Martha Lorans was rapidly flipping through some tapes. It looked, to an outsider, like she was quickly scanning, searching for something she wished to read. The two men, as usual, had their heads over a battlechess game.

Helen said to Martha, "What are you sopping up?"

Martha looked at her, her eyes at first blank, but then clearing as she came into the here and now. "How to run this spaceship," she said.

The little girl winced. "Let's hope it doesn't come to that."

Martha laughed. As always, on her it looked particularly good. "You never know," she said. "There is very little knowledge that is worthless."

"Look, how about you going to the captain and sending a space cable to Avalon for me?" Helen said quickly.

Doctor Horsten looked up and scowled at her. "Avalon? Why?"

"I want to buy in on a development there."

They were all looking at her now. She looked down at her little girl shoes, and appeared like nothing so much as an eight-year-old asking for some privilege she highly suspected was going to be denied.

She added, "I have some interplanetary credit savings banked in the exchange computers on Earth. I'd like to have them transferred to Avalon and invested in the Sky-High Development Corporation."

Lorans' eyes narrowed. "Why?"

"Oh, I just want to."

Doctor Horsten nodded sourly. "What is this corporation?"

"Oh, it's just in the process of being organized."

"Ummm. And why is it you're so anxious to buy in?"

"Oh, there've been a few rumors around the ship."

Horsten shook his head. "You little sneak. I saw you playing with your doll under the table of those two sharpies from Avalon. Now look here, if Martha did make such a purchase then those two businessmen would know there'd been a leak on this ship. The Lorans family would come under suspicion. And we don't want anybody to start wondering about the Lorans family, nor their friend, Doctor Horsten."

"Little sneak," she snorted. "Why, you big ox. I ought to clobber you."

Martha Lorans laughed. "I'd like to see that some day. But Dorn's right, Helen."

Little Helen snorted again, but jumped up into one of the lounge's chairs and spread her skirt neatly, the way a precocious child spreads her skirt.

She snarled under her breath, "What the hell's the use of getting onto a good thing, if you're not allowed to profit by it? I could triple my interplanetary credits."

The others had gone back to their pursuits.

After a few minutes, Helen sighed and said, "Martha, how about reciting that bit about the bullfighting again."

Martha looked up. "All of it?"

"Not all the details about the history of the bullfight. I still don't believe it! A relic of the Roman arena coming all the way down to the present—at least on Falange. And imagine those cloddies going to the trouble of freighting enough of these—what was the name of the breed of bull they have to ship all the way from Mother Earth, Martha?"

"*Bos taurus ibericus.*"

"Right . . . and they're useless for anything except the so-called fiesta brava."

"Well," Horsten said, "it's still their national spectacle,

their national fascination. Evidently, every Falangist on the planet is an *aficionado,* a bullfight buff."

Helen said in disgust, "But using it as a method of picking a Chief of State! When the Caudillo dies, that matador pronounced *Numero Uno* becomes the new Caudillo. Why, that's chaos! Nothing to do with education or intelligence quotient . . . nothing to do with background in governing . . . nothing to do with anything— except bullfighting! There's nothing so silly in the whole of United Planets."

"I don't know," Pierre Lorans said. "There's some pretty silly methods of selecting those who govern, including a hereditary monarchy." He looked thoughtful. "A top matador would have to be in physically fine shape. He'd have to be sharp, quick, or he would never have become *Numero Uno.* He couldn't be stupid—a stupid person with good reflexes might survive in the ring for a time, but occasions would come up when he could save himself from disaster only by utilizing intelligence."

"Anything for an argument, eh?" Helen snorted. "Defending the silliest method of selecting a dictator that's ever come down the pike."

Dorn Horsten put down the piece he was holding and said thoughtfully, "What I can't understand is why the elite exposes itself to the danger of having one of the underprivileged class win control. No power elite ever willingly gives up its position. Why, if the wrong man got in there—wrong from their view—he could upset their applecart for all time."

Martha said, or rather recited, "Our information on this aspect of Falange government is scanty. It would seem that one of the factors that keeps the average Falangist

37

contented with the status quo is that every person on the planet, theoretically, has the chance to become the Caudillo. When the old Caudillo dies, a celebration sweeps the planet. For weeks, during which the fights are being held and contestants being eliminated, the planet Falange is in a state of euphoria difficult to conceive of on the part of anyone who has not witnessed it."

"That's a point," Dorn Horsten said. "If you condone the system, and even enjoy it, and especially if you take part yourself, or support a friend, relation or comrade in the fights, you can hardly protest the system later." He took up the chess piece again and muttered thoughtfully, "I still can't imagine the Falange powers that be taking the chance of a peasant or unskilled worker becoming Caudillo."

Helen evidently grew suddenly bored and bounced down from her chair. "I think I'll go pester Ferd," she announced.

Dorn Horsten scowled at her. "Why?" Then added, "Who?"

Martha looked at Helen. "You mean that brain surgeon?"

"Ferdinand Zogbaum," Helen said. "But he's not a brain surgeon, he's some sort of electronics wizard."

"Not necessarily mutually exclusive," Horsten said seriously. "What is the attraction of Citizen Zogbaum?"

Helen giggled. "Well, for one thing, he's the nearest thing to a man my size on board."

Pierre Lorans looked at her accusingly. "Pester him, is right. I saw you sitting on his lap yesterday, pulling at the poor cloddy's cravat, and him trying to carry on a serious conversation with the second officer."

Helen said, "He's cute."

Martha snorted. "Cute! He looks like nothing so much as a half-sized Lincoln."

Helen started out the compartment entry. She said over her shoulder, "If he'd stop wearing those elevator heels, he'd be almost just right."

Pierre looked after her and said thoughtfully, "That little witch is going to make a mistake and bust up the whole act one of these days."

Horsten shrugged. "It must be difficult for her. She can't allow herself to be seen participating in any adult activity. How would you like to be in a spot where you couldn't even read—except for children's tapes."

V

On his way out from Commissioner Ross Metaxa's office, Derek Lamb stopped at Irene Karansky's desk and said, "Irene, there are some things I need, mostly forged identification papers, for my current assignment."

She looked up at him from her work and said snappishly, "What do you think I am, a one woman department? You know where to go for forged papers."

He was shaking his head. "This one is so confidential that we must have as few in on it as possible. We can't afford any sort of a leak."

She eyed him. "Where are you going?"

He shook his head again. "I don't want even you to know that, Irene."

She snorted. "You *are* being secretive. All right, I'll put the whole job in the hands of only one man. What do you need?"

"A passport from the planet Lenin. Very authentic looking. My face, fingerprints and so forth. An exit visa from Lenin in it and an entry visa to Earth. Then I'll want an interplanetary credit card with a balance of roughly, but not exactly, fifty thousand credits. I'll want various other papers that a man ordinarily carries, perhaps an identity card showing me to be a, say, Colonel Inspector in some police sounding organization, with a communist name. Possibly, there'll be some personal letters from my wife. Give her a Russian name, Catherina, or something."

"Wait a minute," Irene said. "I don't think there is a planet named Lenin, either in United Planets or out of it."

"I know. I just invented it. Locate it, in my papers, in a sector as far away on the star charts from Stalin as possible. Can you think of a good Russian sounding name for me?"

Irene thought about it. "How about Ilya Simonov? I just read a historical fiction novel about a Russian espionage-counterespionage agent with that name."

"Okay, that'll do. Remember these papers have to look absolutely authentic, or my name will be mud. I'm going over to the historical archives. You can find me there, if you need me."

"That sounds dry as dust," Irene said. "What in the world are you going to do there?"

"Study up on 20th Century communism," Derek told her.

It was only a bit over a week later that Derek pulled up before the Stalin Embassy in Greater Washington, got out of his aircushion taxi and stared up at the building. Judging from the signs, the edifice housed more than one embassy staff. Mostly worlds he had never heard of; probably minor colonies that conducted little interplanetary intercourse and didn't need a very large staff representing them at United Planets.

He was dressed in a style not currently in on Mother

41

Earth, and probably never had been. His conservative suit was dark, heavy and of obviously long-wearing material. His square-toed, husky shoes were black and without a shine.

He entered the door, checked out the location of the Stalin Embassy and took the elevator to the fifth floor. Evidently, the embassy occupied the whole level and by the looks of it included the living quarters of the embassy staff as well as their offices.

The reception room was near the elevator banks and there was what was obviously a guard standing before it. The other sized Derek up at his approach. He was a stolid, square cut, forty-year-old who didn't look as though he had smiled since childhood.

Derek said, "Where would I see about getting a visa for the planet Stalin?"

The other ogled him. "A visa!" He spoke in Earth-basic.

"Yes, of course."

The other shook his head, his expression indicating that now he had heard everything. However, it was not up to him to issue any opinions or statements whatsoever.

He opened the door for the newcomer and said, "You can inquire from the girl at the desk."

The girl at the desk was neat enough, and almost pretty in a cow-like Slavic fashion. But she was clad in the drabbest dress Derek Lamb could offhand ever remember seeing, wore no makeup whatsoever and certainly no jewelry.

Derek Lamb came to a rigid posture before her, as though he had a military background, and said, "Colonel Inspector Ilya Simonov, of the planet Lenin. I have come for a visa to visit Stalin."

She stared at him, her very blue eyes indicating that here was a problem that had never raised its head in the office before.

"I . . . well . . . I . . . what is the purpose of your visit to Stalin?" she said, her voice wavering.

"I would rather not reveal that to you, Comrade, but only to the highest official in your embassy."

"Comrade?" she said.

"Yes, Comrade. I am from Lenin."

"I . . . don't believe I have ever heard of the planet Lenin."

"Also originally settled from the Soviet Complex, Comrade."

"I see." She hesitated, then said, "Kliment Gramatikov, the Ambassador, is in his office. I will check to see if he is available.

She did and he was.

The embassy offices were even smaller and fewer in number than Derek Lamb had thought at first. The ambassador's room was immediately off this one. The girl had gone over to a door to open it for the newcomer. She let him pass through and closed it behind him.

The ambassador was seated behind the desk. He was a rolypoly type with a completely bald head which looked as though it was shaved daily. Derek Lamb had never seen a shaved head before, not in these days of renewing hair.

Derek put his heels together and said formally, "Colonel Inspector Ilya Simonov, Comrade Ambassador, requesting a visa to visit Stalin."

The other stared at him, as the girl, and the guard before. He blurted, "But we grant no visas to visit Stalin, Colonel."

"I am an exception. I have been sent by the government of Lenin, on a mission to your planet."

"What kind of a mission?" The ambassador had never heard of the planet Lenin any more than the receptionist had but he wasn't about to admit that.

"That, Comrade, I am free to disclose only to Alex Vavilov, Chairman of the Presidium of your Central Committee," Derek said, his voice firm.

Ambassador Gramatikov finally got out, "Your credentials, please."

Derek Lamb brought forth his forged passport and handed it over with his police identity card.

He said, "My Lenin passport and my credentials as a Colonel Inspector in the *Chrzvychainaya Kommissiya*."

The ambassador was surprised. "You have, then, as on Stalin, an Extraordinary Commission for Combating CounterRevolution, Sabotage and Speculation?"

"Yes, of course. Sometimes called the *Cheka*. Our government is modelled after that which prevailed in the days of Vladimir Ilich Ulyanov, N. Lenin, in short."

The ambassador fished in his desk and came up with a bottle two thirds full of a colorless liquid and two glasses. "Please be seated Comrade Colonel Inspector." He added, "A glass of vodka?"

"Of course. Thank you very much. I am anxious to compare your vodka with that of Lenin. We pride ourselves on our vodka," Derek said.

The ambassador poured for them both and took up his glass. "To the Proletarian Dictatorship," he toasted.

"Long live the Revolution," Derek told him.

They knocked the fiery spirit back and the ambassador poured again but returned to perusing the passport before taking the second drink.

44

SECTION G: UNITED PLANETS

"Excellent vodka," Derek said.

The ambassador nodded his appreciation of the compliment and said, "I have heard little of what is obviously a sister planet, your Lenin, but I see from your coordinates that you are at the far side of United Planets from us."

"That is correct, Comrade."

"And you are sure, Comrade Colonel Inspector Simonov, that you are unable to give me even a hint as to your reason for interviewing Comrade Vavilov?"

"I am afraid not." Derek allowed his voice to go a bit stiff. "It is top secret, Comrade."

Gramatikov sighed. "Very well," he said. "Unfortunately, I am not empowered to give you a visa for landing on Stalin, Comrade Simonov. The most I can do from here is issue you permission to disembark on the satellite above our planet. There, local authorities will meet you and rule on the question."

Derek picked up his drink and tossed it back. "Very well, Comrade. At least that takes me one step nearer to my goal."

VI

At the knock on his partly ajar door, Sid Jakes called, "Come in, come on in. It's open. It's always open." He looked up expectantly.

And frowned.

The little man said hesitantly, "Supervisor Jakes?"

Sid Jakes said, "Ah, come in. Take a chair. Excuse me for a minute."

While the colorless newcomer settled down, hands folded in lap, Sid Jakes flicked on his orderbox screen. "Irene," he complained. "Didn't I tell you I was expecting a top priority——"

The screen squawked back and Sid Jakes flinched. He grinned. "All right, all right, I love you too. But the thing is, I'm sure this—" he looked over at the newcomer, "—ah, gentleman has something very important. If he got past you, it better be something important. However, I am momentarily expecting one of Li Chang's new Special Talent agents and——"

The orderbox screen squawked.

Sid Jakes did a double take.

He switched off the interoffice communicator and said accusingly, "You're Sam?"

The other flushed with embarrassment and nodded.

Sid Jakes closed his eyes for a long moment. His face worked slightly. He shook his head finally. He opened his eyes again, hopefully.

He said, "Cosmetics and Wardrobe have certainly done a fine job on you, ah Citizen. . . ."

"Goodboy," the other squeaked. He cleared his throat apologetically.

"I beg your pardon?" Sid Jakes said. He had the damnedest feeling that every other sentence was being left out of this conversation. Either that or he had come in too late to get the beginning.

"Goodboy," the other said. "Samuel Goodboy."

"Oh," Sid Jakes said, forcing heartiness into his voice. "Well, they certainly did a good job on you. You'll snake past the Dorian immigration and police like——"

"Who?" the little man said.

Jakes looked at him. "Who what?"

"Pardon me. I meant, who did the job on me?"

"The Wardrobe and Plastic Surgery people over in the Department of Dirty Tricks."

Sam Goodboy looked at him blankly.

Sid Jakes said, "Oh, no."

It was the newcomer's turn to say, "I beg your pardon?"

"Never mind," Jakes said painfully. "Li Chang is our most astute recruiter. She's never pulled a bad fling yet." He took in the other again and repeated, "Yet."

"Yes, sir," Goodboy said apologetically. He looked as though he'd go about a hundred and ten pounds, sopping wet, with a suitcase in his hand. And from his facial expression, it was obvious that he was apologetic about being alive.

Jakes looked at him for a long time. Finally, he took

47

a deep breath and said, "All right, here's the assignment." Something came to him and he said, "This is your first?"

"Oh, yes."

Sid Jakes blinked. "You've never even been on a minor assignment as somebody's assistant, or something? Something to, well, kind of blood you?"

"No, sir." The little man swallowed. "Supervisor Chu just signed me up last week."

"Last *week!* What kind of training have you been through?"

"Training?"

Sid Jakes counted down for a moment or two. Then "Look, ah, Goodboy. In the old days it would take up to five years to turn out a Section G operative. A couple of years just to locate a potential with the required mental and physical elements, and the dedication."

"Oh," the other said in a wistful sort of way. "I've got the dream. The United Planets dream."

The Section G higher-up ignored him. "Then another three years of training and apprentice level work. Most didn't make it. It took a lot to become a full-fledged agent, complete with bronze badge, not to speak of Special Agent with silver badge."

"Oh, I've got a badge," the other said proudly. His hand fumbled over his pockets. He frowned apologetically. "I'm sure I had it right here . . . somewhere."

Sid Jakes closed his eyes again. When he opened them, the little fellow was displaying a bronze badge, lettered simply, *Samuel Goodboy, Section G, Bureau of Investigation, United Planets*. It seemed to glow in the small, inoffensive man's hand.

"Who gave you that?"

"Why, Supervisor Chu."

"Oh, she did. After recruiting you only last week?" The other nodded.

"Well, you can tell Supervisor . . ." Sid Jakes broke it off. "No, sir," he said. "I won't do it. She's sucked me in on others in the Special Talents gang of hers. If Li Chang says that you're an assassin, I'll ride along with her until she takes a Brody. She's issued you a communicator and a Model H Gun?"

"No, I'm afraid of guns."

There was another long silence. Sid Jakes looked at the much smaller man, and had the damnedest feeling that he'd like to squat down on the floor and contemplate his navel.

Sam Goodboy said, "She didn't think I ought to take a Section G communicator with me. Or anything else they might detect. There's only one spaceport on Doria and the police are ever so sharp about detecting anything like a weapon, or anything like a Section G communicator."

Sid grunted. "She's right, as usual." His built-in optimism fought its way to the surface. "Undoubtedly, that's where your special talent comes in. You've got a better way of assassinating El Primero than with an ordinary gun. But we'll get to that later. First, let me give you a rundown on the assignment."

He settled back in his chair. "Down through the ages, we've always had assassins. In the past, no man in power could adequately defend himself against a really dedicated assassin. The very term comes from an organization which, high on Indian hemp, pulled off some of the more notable political killings on record.

Jakes began warming to his tale. "The story is told

that Richard the Lion Heart was first inclined to give Hasan Ben Sabbah, the Old Man of the Mountain, and head of the assassin sect, a hard time. But when he awoke one morning, there was a knife on the pillow next to him. He doubled his guard, but the next morning there was another knife. In a rage, he again doubled his security. And the next morning, another knife. Richard made his peace with Hasan Ben Sabbah."

"Yes, Supervisor," the other said.

"Then there were the Nihilists of Russia; at least some of them, one wing of the organization. They were convinced they could scare the aristocracy into granting reforms. They were wrong, for various reasons, but they tried. They thought that individuals were at the root of Russian evils. They pulled off some noteworthy assassinations, sometimes blowing up whole trains to get a Czar or a Grand Duke."

Sid Jakes shook his head. "No, in the past, a political figure had no chance against a determined, organized group which wished to assassinate him. Even individuals could pull it off, given determination, since a political figure could not avoid the public. To maintain contact with people, he had to show himself. Take the American presidents, for example. Lincoln, at the theatre, killed by a single man—Booth. McKinley, again in public, shaking hands with a long line of people. The anarchist, Czolgosz, approached with a hand supposedly in a bandage, actually concealing a gun. The first Kennedy, driving in a procession; once again, killed by an individual."

Sam Goodboy said, "Yes, sir. You make your point." He cleared his throat. "Ah, what is your point?"

Sid Jakes scowled at him. How in the name of Holy

Jumping Zen could Li Chang have ever turned up this cloddy in recruiting Section G operatives?

However, he went on. "The point is that almost invariably, before, the ruler, the victim of assassination, was hit by the assassin while appearing in public, a duty he could not avoid." He paused. "Today, it is no longer necessary. Since the advent of radio, television, and now Tri-D, the public figure no longer need appear *in person* to the people. And today, such potential victims of the assassin as El Primero, never, but never, leave the security of their quarters."

Sam Goodboy nodded, and tried to project earnest intelligence, failing miserably.

Sid Jakes said, "El Primero's defense is as strong as any the human race has ever seen. If our information is correct, he has a method, utilizing brain surgery and psychedelic drugs, of insuring the total faithfulness of his bodyguard and those connected with his security. They are incapable of being seduced by his enemies, incapable of betraying him. The first troupe we sent to undermine his regime, made that mistake."

Sam swallowed. "He had them shot?"

"No. He had them treated. After spilling everything they knew about Section G and the workings of United Planets, they became members of his bodyguard and hold that position now."

"Oh."

Sid Jakes went on. "So we sent in another troupe. This one with orders to bring El Primero down, whatever. They decided to get him from a distance and set up some special weapons from our Department of Dirty Tricks."

51

"And?"

"The first troupe, now faithful members of Michael Ortega's bodyguard, knew all about such special weapons. The second group was captured by the first and became part of his bodyguard, too."

Sam winced. "You said that three troupes preceded me."

"Yes. We finally went the whole hog and sent three of our top men, headed by Ronny Bronston, our best field man. We lost communication with them last week."

"And?"

"And assume they're either dead or now part of El Primero's bodyguard, completely devoted to him." Sid Jakes let a flash of his characteristic humor, albeit a bit on the sour side, come through. "So now, after the expenditure of ten of our veteran agents, we have you, Sam. With one week of seniority to your credit."

"Yes, sir," Sam said cooperatively.

"And now, would you tell me just what this neat trick of yours is? Why did Li Chang Chu made you an agent after only one week of, uh, training?"

"Yes, sir. My special talent is I can kill people." He cleared his throat. "People, or anything else."

"*How?*" Sid Jakes blurted.

"I think them to death."

VII

The arrival at the Nuevo Madrid spaceport, the only entry point to Falange, was even less eventful than they had hoped for. Their coming, of course, was anticipated. Securing a visa at the Falange Embassy on Terra was no everyday matter. No one, but no one, arrived unannounced on Falange.

There was a delegation of biochemists from the University, breathless at meeting the celebrated Doctor Dorn Horsten. He was hustled off to a group of horse-drawn *carruajes*.

The Lorans family looked after him.

"Holy Ultimate," Helen said under her breath. "I never expected to see a landau pulled by a span of horses anywhere except in a Tri-Di historical."

"Well, get ready to ride in one," Martha told her. "It seems to be the latest method of local transportation."

They were being approached by what were obviously customs and immigration officials, done up in costumes seemingly out of Nineteenth Century Iberia, and by two civilians who looked like diplomats of the Victorian period.

"Here we go," Pierre Lorans said. He puffed his cheeks up and went into his Gallic facial expression.

Helen said to Martha, her voice still low, "Look. Evidently, Ferd Zogbaum has been snagged by the local fuzz."

Martha turned her eyes in the indicated direction. The young electronics engineer, or whatever he was, was being marched in the direction of some very military-looking buildings at the far end of the field. The guards, in their *Guardia Civil* uniforms, complete with hard, black hats, were, however, carrying his bags.

Martha said, "Probably some minor technicality in his papers. He doesn't seem to be particularly worried." Their own delegation was nearly upon them. Martha's voice changed in caliber. "Now sweetie, be quiet for awhile. Mummie and Daddy have to talk to these nice gentlemen."

"Curd," Helen said under her breath.

The uniformed men, after well-executed bows and murmered politeness, took over passports, interplanetary health cards and the rest of the red-tape documents involved in aliens landing upon the planet Falange. The civilians, it turned out, were members of the cultural affairs department of the Caudillo's government.

While the papers were being perused and stamped, they made meaningless conversation and minor gushings of welcome. When the papers were obviously approved, the gushing became more pronounced.

Martha even got her hand kissed.

In a sudden childish burst of enthusiasm, Helen jumped up and put her arms around one of the official's neck, her sturdy little legs about his waist.

"Oh, isn't he a *nice* man!"

Martha said, "Helen!"

The cultural aide blinked, smiled in attempted accept-

54

ance, and put his hands under the little girl's bottom, as though to support her weight. The vaguest of incomprehensive expressions crossed his face momentarily—as though he hadn't expected the bottom to feel quite the way it did.

Pierre Lorans grabbed Helen and pulled her away. "Don't be so impulsive, chocolate drop," he scolded.

Evidently, the Earth Embassy of Falange had forwarded full information on the highly noted Nouveau Cordon Bleu chef, Pierre Lorans. It was a pleasure to welcome such an artist of haute cuisine to Falange. It was thought possible that he would be invited to an audience with El Caudillo himself.

El Caudillo was extremely fond of Basque cuisine. Perhaps Senor Lorans . . . ?

Senor Lorans puffed out his cheeks. "Gentlemen, I am perhaps the most proficient preparer of *bacalao a la vizcaina* and *anguilas a la bilbaina* in all the United Planets."

The one who had introduced himself as Manola Camino, looked blank. "But, Senor Lorans, we have neither codfish nor eels on Falange. These dishes we know of only through tradition and the writings brought with us from Earth."

Lorans glared at him in indignation. "No *bacalao*, no *anguilas*! Are you barbarians? How can your . . . ah . . . Caudillo, or whatever you call him, be a connoisseur of Basque food if you have no *bacalao*, no *anguilas*?" He sneered openly. "Next you will tell me you have no beans for *fabada*!"

The Falangist winced, opened his mouth unhappily, then closed it again.

55

The other cultural aide said hurriedly, "Perhaps we had better proceed to the Posada."

They led the way, the Loranses trailing after.

Martha said from the side of her mouth, "Listen, you show-off, aren't you overdoing it?"

"No," he whispered back. "It's all in character."

Helen skipped as they went, singing, in her tinkle of a child's voice, something about three little girls in blue, tra la, three little girls in blue.

Senor Manola Camino led the way to two of the horse-drawn carriages which seemed the local equivalent of taxis and they were shortly underway. There were comparatively few powered vehicles on the streets of Nuevo Madrid, and it seemed that these few must be imports and almost exclusively for police, military, and, perhaps, the highest ranking authorities. The planet Falange as a whole lived in the day of the horse.

It seemed, also, that the Posada San Francisco was the only hotel in the city that catered to aliens. Either that, or it was the best hostelry in town and VIPs were automatically taken there. At any rate, they could see Doctor Horsten at the desk, still surrounded by his bevy of welcoming scientists. And while they went through their own routine of registering, they saw Ferdinand Zogbaum enter, still accompanied by his two policemen.

Their schedule didn't begin until the next day, when Lorans was to have a tour of the leading restaurants of Nuevo Madrid. As soon as they were delivered to their suite, and their guides had bowed their way out, they began to make the usual sounds of unpacking.

The rooms were monstrous in size; a living room, two bedrooms and a rather antiquated bath. The antiquated quality prevailed in general, giving the impression it was deliberately laid on. Even the furniture was Victorian in design. The ceiling was more than thrice as high as could have been expected in population-packed Earth and there was actually a wood-burning fireplace.

While Martha and Helen did the unpacking, Pierre made a tour of the suite, jabbering along as he went.

"Now dear," Martha said shrilly, "please stay out of Mother's way."

Helen snarled softly at her.

Pierre said, "Did you hear that drivel? Do they think me a dunderhead? How can one cook in the fashion of the Basques without *bacalao*?"

"Now dear, you know perfectly well they were very pleasant. And it was nice to meet us out there on that terrible expanse of cement and all."

Helen shrilled, "Three little girls in blue, tra la. Three little girls in blue!"

Pierre spotted what he was looking for, at the very top of the chain from which the chandelier was suspended. Right at the ceiling, a good twenty feet above them. He pointed and they looked up.

There was no apparent way in which any of them could reach the bug. No combination of furniture, piled atop each other. Martha nodded to Pierre.

Pierre Lorans took a ballbearing from his pocket. Seconds later, he said with satisfaction, "I doubt if there's any more."

Helen said, "Look, for a day or two we're going to be safe. They won't get around to suspecting a thing, not even a broken bug. And until tomorrow, when you'll have your time monopolized, we're free. We better get busy tonight."

"At what?" Martha said. "They didn't give us a clue

57

on how we were to begin this big subversion bit, back on Earth. You'd think Jakes would have something for us to start with. Somebody to see."

Helen snapped chubby fingers. "That's it. We've got to find the local underground."

Pierre Lorans looked at her. "Wonderful. How do we go about that? What local underground?"

"There must be one. Given any government at all and there's some opposition. It might be large or it might be small, but somewhere on Falange there's an underground."

Martha said slowly, "You're probably right, but how we get in touch is another thing. If the *Policia Secreta* can't find them, how can we?"

Something came to Helen. "Those former three agents from Section G. What was it Sid Jakes said happened to them?"

Martha's eyes took on their empty look. She recited, *"In each case they were unmasked, in one manner or the other, and brought to trial on trumped up charges. One was accused of murder, one of subversion and the other disrespect of the Caudillo; all capital offenses."*

"Okay," Helen said, an edge of excitement in her voice. "That's it. One of them was charged with subversion. A man doesn't commit subversion on his own. He works with a group, a party, an underground organization of some sort or other."

"So?" Lorans scowled.

"So that Section G operative wasn't tried alone. There has to be others involved. Others captured at the same time. It's almost sure to be."

"Perhaps," Martha said. "But, if so, what of it? Surely they've all been executed by now."

"Not necessarily," Helen insisted. "They would execute the Section G agent quickly before United Planets took some measure to free him. But their own citizens they might keep alive in hopes of squeezing information out of them."

"Hmmm," Lorans said.

Martha said, "But what of it?"

"Don't you see? Somewhere there are trial records. If we can get hold of them, we can locate where these companions of our Section G agent are. What prison they're in."

Martha and Pierre Lorans were both unhappy now. They considered it.

"We don't even know where the court records might be—if there are any," Pierre objected. "For all we know, the trial was secret."

Helen said decisively, "That's for you to find out. This afternoon take a guided tour. Those cultural department aides are just dying to show you the sights. Among them will be the Caudillo's palace, the post office, the museum and city hall. If you can, worm out of them just where the archives are. It shouldn't be too hard if you blather along like usual sightseers. And the Holy Ultimate knows, no two persons in United Planets can blather like you two."

Pierre Lorans aimed a backhanded swipe at her, knowing perfectly well it would never connect.

Helen bounced back, tinkling laughter.

Martha said, "How about you?"

"Tell them I'm tired and don't want to leave the hotel. You might even hint it's a relief to get away from me, after the long trip. Meanwhile, I'll see Dorn and tell him what's up."

59

SECTION G: UNITED PLANETS

Martha and Pierre Lorans looked at each other. "I can't think of anything else," he admitted.

Helen was already out of the room and on her way down to the lobby.

She met Ferdinand Zogbaum coming up the wide stairway, the two police officers and several bellhops with luggage trailing after him.

She grabbed him about the waist and squealed, "Uncle Ferd, Uncle Ferd, why are these nasty policemen always following you all around!"

Martha had been right. Ferdinand Zogbaum looked like nothing so much as the youthful Lincoln, cut down to half size. In short, no beauty, if you ignored the wistful sadness in his face. Now he was flushing. He looked apologetically over his shoulder at the two guards. The whole party had ground to a halt under the child's assault.

He patted her on the head. "Now, now, Helen. I'm not being arrested. They're friends."

"They're policemen," Helen shrilled. "Mommy told me they were policemen. Why are they following you, Uncle Ferd?"

One of the guards was grinning in amusement, the other looked bored.

Ferd Zogbaum cleared his throat unhappily and patted her head again. "They're guarding me, honey. Don't you worry. Your Uncle Ferd is a very important man brought all the way from Mother Earth for a special job, so he had to have these big policemen guard him so he can't come to any harm."

"Is that straight?" she said under her breath.

He blinked. "What?"

"I love you, Uncle Ferd," she said, her voice high

60

again. "You be sure you say goodbye to me before you go anywhere away from the hotel. Or I'll go run to the United Planets Embassy and tell everybody you've been kidnapped. I can lie real good."

The bored guard became animated enough to scowl.

Ferd said, "Don't worry. If I leave here I'll say goodbye to you first."

She pressed her full, cupid bow lips to his mouth, released him and headed down the steps again. For a moment, he looked after her, a strange look on his face. That was the damnedest child's kiss he had ever received. But then he shook his head unbelievingly and resumed his way to his suite, followed by his entourage.

VIII

It was more than a month before Derek Lamb was able to secure passage to the planet Stalin. He spent the time boning up on the Russia of Lenin and Stalin and found it a chore. Offhand, he had seldom run into so chaotic a politicoeconomic system, and in United Planets you had some pretty chaotic ones.

So far as he could figure out, no matter what Lenin might originally have had in mind, toward the end of his days, and through all of the Stalin period, what the Russians had finally come up with was a system of State Capitalism. Far from going to the classless society they supposedly advocated, they built their New Class of Party bureaucrats. Far from letting the State wither away, as Karl Marx had said it would, they strengthened it. Far from abolishing such capitalist institutions as the wages system, banking, money and interest, and all the rest of basic capitalist institutions, they maintained them. The top communist bureaucrats lived like millionaires, and the bottom peasants and workers like Alabama cotton-pickers.

Finally the day for departure arrived. The Space Ship *Goddard,* out of the planet Catalina, set down on Earth. A freighter, with accommodations for a few passengers, she was en route to, among other remote planets, Stalin. Catalina was a fairly progressive, industrial feudalistic planet, which specialized considerably in interplanetary commerce. She had several thousand space freighters continually plying between the worlds.

Somewhat to his surprise, Derek found himself to be the only passenger, at least on this leg of the journey. The *Goddard* evidently didn't hit the United Planets worlds where tourism was popular or commerce thriving. It specialized in out-of-the-way ports; sometimes really-out-of-the-way worlds—such as Stalin.

He ate at Captain Simack's table, but so did everybody else on board, save the ordinary spacemen. And he killed time reading and playing battlechess with the skipper. Captain Simack beat him all ways from Tuesday, finally winding up with spotting Derek two tanks and a machinegun nest at each game. The captain of the *Goddard* had nothing to do with his leisure time save play battlechess. There is no more boring travel than that in space. Nothing to see and nothing to do, save self-entertainment.

The skipper was obviously intrigued by Ilya Simonov and did his best to worm out of him that which was to be wormed.

Between moves, Simack said, "You know, I've never known of a case of someone landing on Stalin. You'd think they were afraid of rats, bearing plague fleas."

"Ummm, so I understand," Derek said, moving a tank in an attempt to corner the other's Field Marshal. "What do you know about Stalin? You've made this run before?"

"Oh, yes." The skipper countered the move, more than successfully.

Derek studied the battlefield. He was in for it.

"But never landed, eh?" he said. "What do you think of the citizens that you meet up on the satellite?"

"Zombis," the captain snorted. He was a big man, obviously long, long in the space service of Catalina and probably looking forward, somewhat wistfully, if not desperately, to his pension. He had a hard mouth, and hard, tired eyes, and although he was perfectly correct with his sole passenger, Derek would have hated to have to serve under him.

Any additional information Derek could accumulate about Stalin might prove priceless later, though he doubted that the captain had much to offer.

He said, "I'm surprised that you stop there at all. I had gained the impression that the planet was self sufficient, not needing interplanetary commerce."

The captain moved a piece then muttered sour humor. He said, "There's one phenomenon in the colonization of space that you run into over and over again, Simonov. Nostalgia."

Derek looked at him. "Nostalgia? What's that got to do with the spaceship's stopping at Stalin's satellite?"

The captain laughed. "Take the Chinese who settled Han. You know the one thing they import? Soy sauce. They import it by the tanker load. It seems that you can't raise decent soy beans on the planet Han, and the Chinese can't face existence without soy sauce. With the French who colonized New Paris, it's snails. No snails on New Paris, so they'll pay for them in their weight in gold."

Derek rubbed his front teeth with his right forefinger. "I still——"

The captain said, "With the Russians on Stalin it's caviar, smoked sturgeon and smoked salmon. They can't raise the fish on their own planet, so they import it from Mother Earth."

"Caviar!" Derek blurted. "Isn't that a little on the expensive side for a planet like Stalin?"

The skipper laughed his sour laugh again, even as he eyed the board. He was moving in for the kill, and Derek's Field Marshal was on the run.

He said, "That's something you'll find on these dictatorship worlds. Very seldom do those who do the dictating live the staid life. Stalin is no exception. The bureaucrats do just fine."

He looked up at Derek. "Come to think of it, your passport listed you as from Lenin. Sounds as though a planet with a name like that might possibly have a communist dictatorship as well."

Derek didn't answer that. He pretended to study the board.

The captain said gently. "There's just one difficulty about that suggestion." There was a quizzical element in his voice.

Derek brought his eyes up to the other's.

The captain said, "There is no planet Lenin."

Derek said evenly, "Lenin is not a member of United Planets."

"I know it isn't. And it's not one of the non-member worlds, either. Mr. Simonov, I've been in space since I was a kid. I've traveled in every sector of the galaxy that the human race has colonized. I don't mean that I've necessarily landed on every colonized world, but I've at least passed fairly near. And I know this—there is no planet Lenin."

Derek Lamb sized him up for a long moment before saying, "So?"

The captain made a move which wound up the game. Derek's Field Marshal wasn't yet checkmated, but it was only a matter of a move or two. He was going to have to concede.

The other said, "I bear you no ill will, Simonov. But if I were you I'd think twice about landing on Stalin —even if they give you permission. That planet's been a police state for a long time. They know every trick in the totalitarian book—probably including whatever trick you're trying to pull on them."

"Thanks," Derek said. "I concede."

The planet Stalin was amazingly Earth-like, actually to within only a few degrees, in the system they used for comparison. It had one large continent, two smaller ones, a multitude of islands and, like Mother Earth, was largely covered by ocean. It was one damn nice world, Derek Lamb decided before ever setting down on it.

The artificial satellite which circled Stalin was, in actuality, a converted space freighter of obsolete design. Circled wasn't quite the term. It remained stationary over the capital city, Stalingrad. It turned out to be crewed by a mere handful and Derek gained the impression that if more manpower was needed temporarily, when a cargo ship came in, they were shuttled up from the planet below.

Captain Simack was an artist. He warped into and made contact with the satellite so carefully, so precisely, that Derek Lamb could hardly detect when initial contact was made.

The captain, the third officer of the *Goddard,* and Derek were the only three to cross over, through the space hatches, to the converted freighter. On the way, they passed three Stalinists—customs and health officials —on their way to check out the incoming freighter. All nodded, but no one spoke. All was routine.

The captain said to Derek, from the side of his mouth, "This is your last chance, Simonov, if that's your real name. If you wish, you can continue on with us to Avalon."

"Thanks," Derek said, noncommittally.

"It's your ass, not mine," Simack said with a sigh.

They were met at the satellite portal by three more Stalinists. Two of them were concerned with the cargo of Earth-side delicacies that the *Goddard* had transported. The other was in uniform; a uniform Derek vaguely remembered from historical Tri-Di films. Russian. On the collar were pips proclaiming the other's rank to be major, if Derek remembered correctly.

He remembered correctly. The other brought his heels together, saluted crisply and said, his voice as empty as the space Derek had been traveling through, "Colonel Inspector Ilya Simonov?"

Being in mufti, Derek didn't answer the salute, of course. He said merely, "Yes, Comrade."

"Major Frol Kulski," the other said. "Will you follow me, Colonel?" he turned and led the way.

Derek didn't like the fact that the other hadn't called him comrade. But possibly it meant nothing. Undoubtedly, the other wanted to check him out before expressing any comradely feelings.

The self-named Major Frol Kulski led him to what had probably been the officer's mess and lounge, back in the days when the satellite had been an averagely large space freighter. On their way, they passed various members of the crew. Derek's snap judgement was that they looked competent enough, even efficient. In fact, if anything, they appeared a bit snappier than did the major. He couldn't quite put his finger upon it, but the major seemed a bit on the dull side.

In the officer's mess, his guide went over to an auto-bar refrigerator, saying over his shoulder, "A vodka, Colonel?"

"Of course." Derek found himself a seat at one of the tables.

The other returned with a chill bottle and two three-ounce shot glasses.

Derek said, as the other poured, "I had the pleasure of sampling your vodka at your embassy on Mother Earth. Excellent. I hope to have the opportunity to invite you to test our own from Lenin, some day."

"Unlikely," the other said, lifting his glass in toast. "To the Dictatorship of the Proletariat," he said.

"Long live the Revolution," Derek told him in return as they both tossed their drinks back.

It was one of the sillier bits of business that Derek had picked up in his researches into matters communist. But evidently it was a toast going back to the old days. He would have thought that even the most devout red would have wanted the Revolution to be over as soon as possible, and get on with the building of their dream society, not to see the Revolution prolonged.

The major got to business. "We have had a tight-beam communication from our embassy to United Planets. It is, by the way, the only embassy we maintain."

"So I understand," Derek said. "Part of my mission is to examine the possibilities of an exchange of embassies between our sister planets, Stalin and Lenin."

SECTION G: UNITED PLANETS

The major cleared his throat. "That is not my province, of course."

"Of course."

The major said, "Your credentials, Colonel?"

Derek passed over passport, police identity card, and his interplanetary credit card.

The major poured them more vodka, absently, and began to examine the identity papers. When he got to the interplanetary credit card, his eyebrows went up. "A sizeable credit for one traveling no more than from Lenin to Stalin and return."

Derek tossed back his vodka and, drawing on what he had learned from Captain Simack in regard to the Stalinst bureaucrats doing themselves well, said idly, "We are not poverty-stricken on Lenin. And, besides, my father is a member of the Central Committee."

The major stiffened slightly. "I see," he said. "And rank has its privileges." He licked his lips unhappily and said further, "Comrade Colonel Inspector, it is impossible for you to land on Stalin."

Derek looked at him very coldly. But at least they had got on the comrade salutation basis.

"Those are my instructions, Comrade Colonel Inspector," the major finished.

Derek Lamb's eyes went as bleak as the wastes of that area of Earth once known as Siberia. He said, "I have top secret information for the Chairman of the Presidium."

"What is it?"

"I can't tell you. I am under orders. But the fate of both of our planets lies in the balance."

The major blanched. All over again, Derek decided that he wasn't particularly smart. Kulski took up his glass shakily and put his vodka down without so much as a shudder, though the stuff must have gone at least 100 proof.

He was obviously thinking desperately. He said, "My orders———"

Derek Lamb took a chance. He said, very coldly, "I am not interested in your orders, Major Kulski. I demand to see Alex Vavilov, Chairman of your Presidium. I am under direct orders of Vladimir Mazurov."

"Mazurov?" the other said his face blank.

Which was not surprising, since Derek had made the name up at that very minute.

However, he said, his face and voice colder still, "You have no respect for the leader of the Party on Lenin?"

In a very unmilitary way, the major took a handkerchief from his pocket and wiped his forehead. He said, "I had no idea of the magnitude of your visit."

"It is top secret, which is why I am alone. There are strong forces opposing the Revolution, Comrade."

Major Kulski shakily poured another brace of block busters. This was now going to be nine ounces down the hatch, the Section G man realized, but he up-ended it, as did the other.

Kulski gave up. He said, "You must pardon me, Comrade." At least they were still on the comrade basis, Derek thought. That was a good sign. The other went on. "You must pardon me. I will have to consult with my superiors. Had we known the importance of your mission, I am sure that they would have sent a more ranking comrade or comrades to welcome you."

"Of course," Derek said.

The major came to his feet. "Please remain here for a

few minutes, Comrade. I'll communicate with Stalingrad."

"Of course."

When the other had left, Derek picked up the bottle and poured himself another. He needed it.

IX

Li Chang Chu burst into the office of Irene Kasansky, in a considerable state of excitement.

Irene looked up from her banks of switches and buttons. The dourness faded from her harried face. Supervisor Chu was one of the very few in the department who was immune from the acid of Irene Kasansky. She began a greeting but Li Chang, her face pale, snapped, "I've got to see Commissioner Metaxa."

She had never heard that particular tone from the Chinese supervisor before. She said into one of the orderbox screens, "Shut up, I'll call you back later." She looked up at Li Chang again. "The commissioner is in conference but——"

The feminine supervisor was sweeping past. "With Sid Jakes?"

"Yes, but. . . ." Irene's voice rose. "You can't go in there now. I had definite orders that. . . "

But Li Chang was past her and through the door of the office. Irene Kasansky stared after her.

Ross Metaxa looked up, taken aback as his only female supervisor darted in the door, unannounced. Sloppy of dress, weary of expression, and dissipated in appearance Metaxa might be—but he was a disciplinarian.

Across from him, Sid Jakes lounged, dapper as always, hands in pockets. His eyebrows went up as well. He grinned. "That's what I love about this department," he chortled. "Informality."

"Shut up, you laughing hyena," Metaxa growled. He glowered at Li Chang. "What'd you think this is, the ladies' room? What's the idea of bursting in——"

She ignored him and snapped at Sid Jakes, "Where's Sam?"

"That's a good question. Sam who?"

"Sam Goodboy!"

"Easy, easy," Sid said soothingly. "I took your word for it. Well, not exactly. I made him demonstrate. You know, he killed that fern I had in my office at twenty paces." He grinned and looked over at his superior, who wasn't comprehending all this. "Just by concentrating on it. How's that for a secret weapon? Neat trick, eh?"

Ross Metaxa looked from one of them to the other. "What are you two yokes blithering about?"

Li Chang still ignored the Commissioner of Section G. She said, her voice in agony, to Sid Jakes, "Where is Sam Goodboy?"

Sid Jakes didn't understand as yet. He said happily, "I tested him still further, with a chimp from the zoo. A chimpanzee at a half-mile distance. One minute he was as chipper as——"

"*Where's Sam Goodboy?*"

Jakes broke it off. Both he and Ross Metaxa stared at the diminutive Section G supervisor.

Sid said, "Why, he's on his way to his assignment on Doria. I had him shuttle over to Nuevo Albuquerque yesterday. By now he's on his way."

"Get in contact immediately! Order him back!"

"Order him back?" Jakes said plaintively. "You're the one recommended him. He's gone to crisp old El Primero —couldn't happen to a nicer cloddy—I *can't* get in touch with him. He has no communicator. If he had one, the secret police'd detect it. You know that. They know all about the Section G communicators. He's on his own."

Metaxa roared, "What in the hell is going on here?"

Li Chang sank into a chair, thin shoulders slumped. She said, "Ronny Bronston has broken silence."

"Broken silence," Metaxa said. "He's presumed dead. We haven't heard from him for at least. . . ."

She looked up wearily, and he hushed. "Don't you see what must have happened? Those agents of ours who were captured and treated by Ortega's police—they had communicators. Doria's scientists aren't cloddies. They've obviously been able to analyze the sub-space band we utilized. In other words, tune in on our communciations. Ronny must have found out and discontinued calling us."

Sid Jakes said, "He could have used code."

"Any code is breakable, especially by the stutes on police state worlds."

Ross Metaxa was scowling again. He reached into his desk drawer and brought forth his squat bottle and a glass. He didn't offer any of the clear liquid to his subordinates, knowing better. He knocked a jolt back over his palate, then growled, "Then why did he break silence now?"

There was an embarrassed element in Li Chang's voice. She said, "We . . . that is . . . in our . . . personal relationship . . . well, for amusement, I taught him a few words of Mandarin."

"Mandarin?" Sid Jakes queried.

She looked at him. "Chinese. It's a dead language everywhere except on Han, the planet of my birth."

"Oh," Sid said. Then the meaning came home to him. He laughed. "Their cryptograph people would have to pull a neat trick to decipher that. What'd Ronny say?"

"He only has a few words of Mandarin." She looked down at a note she held in a small hand. "He said . . ." for a moment her voice broke. She took a deep breath and started again. "He said, 'Me take Number One . . . Me change face . . . Me Number One."

They bug-eyed her, speechlessly.

Her eyes went from one to the other in desperation. "Don't you see? Somehow . . . somehow, Ronny has pulled off the biggest romp of his career. He's kidnapped Michael Ortega. He's evidently undergone plastic surgery. Somehow, he's taken El Primero's place."

X

Little Helen skipped into the hotel lobby and up to the desk of the concierge. "Where's my Uncle Dorn?" she trilled.

He looked over the desk and down at her. "Who, Senorita?"

"Uncle Dorn! I want Uncle Dorn."

An inconspicuous type who had been standing at a nearby pillar next to a potted fern, strolled over and murmured to the hotel employee.

"Ah, the Senor Doctor. He has retired to his room, little Senorita."

Helen cocked her blonde head to one side and eyed him speculatively. Finally she said in her childish treble, "What's all this Senorita and Senor jetsam?"

He looked at her a bit startled. "Jetsam?" She looked back at him as unblinkingly as only a child can.

The concierge took a bit of a breath before saying, "Little girl, when our people came from Mother Earth, long, long ago, Earth-basic was already the language all spoke. However, as a concession to our traditions we have maintained a few words of the old tongue. Do you understand?"

"No," Helen said flatly. "Where is my Uncle Dorn?"

The concierge maintained his official aplomb. "He is in Suite A, little Senorita, but I do not think he would wish to be disturbed."

She snorted at that opinion. "He is my Uncle Dorn," she informed him haughtily and headed for the stairs. The concierge shrugged and looked at the inconspicuous representative of the *Policia Secreta* who shrugged as well and obviously forgot about it.

Helen located Suite A and pounded a tiny fist on the door. It was answered by one of the Falange scientists who had met the visiting celebrity at the spaceport. Helen slipped under his arm before he had actually seen her.

Dorn Horsten was seated in a Victorian style easy chair, evidently in the midst of earnest conversation with two of the other local biochemists. They had drinks, in small brandy glasses, at hand.

The famed doctor said, "Ah, the little Princess. Are you also stopping at this hotel, my dear? And how are your good parents. Have you comfortable quarters?"

Helen bent an eye on him, a very blue eye. Obviously, all three questions were of too little importance to require answer. She said, "Uncle Dorn, I want a bedtime story."

"A bedtime story?" He looked at his colleagues in apology, and then out the window. "But, little Princess, it is still only afternoon."

"Mommy and Daddy have gone off to look at the buildings or something and left me all alone to take a nap and I want a story."

"But, Helen," he protested. "I am busy with these gentlemen."

She began to pucker up.

Dorn Horsten made little anxious sounds in his throat

and came to his feet. "Now . . . now . . ." he began.

"I don't like it here in this nasty hotel," she wailed. "I wanna go home!"

"No, now, Helen. Your mother and father will——"

"I wanna bedtime story!" she wailed.

Dorn Horsten looked apologetically at the Falangists. "Senores, if you will pardon me. In actuality, I am a bit weary myself. Perhaps we could postpone our fascinating discussion of the phylum *Thallophyta* until tomorrow."

They had all come to feet before his first three words were out. In moments they were all gone from the room.

Horsten glared down at the diminutive operative and began to say, "What in the . . ."

She had a finger to her lips.

". . . world kind of bedtime story did you have in mind little Princess?"

She sneered at him, held her peace for a moment while her baby blue eyes searched the room. Finally, she located the bug. It was in approximately the same position as the one in the Lorans suite which Pierre had broken with his ball bearing. She pointed it out to him with a chubby finger.

Horsen took off his pince-nez glasses and wiped them, his eyebrows up.

"Would you like the story about Allez Oop?" he said in the tone one uses with an eight-year-old.

"No, no, Uncle Dorn. That's the one you always tell. I want a different one. You come to our room and tell me a different one."

He sighed deeply. "All right, all right, little Princess."

"I'm not so little, Uncle Dorn." As though to prove it, she went over to the table bearing the bottle of cognac, poured herself a hefty slug and knocked it back.

Doctor Dorn Horsten shuddered at the sight. Although he had known her quite a while, it was still difficult to realize that this seeming child was a grown woman. He followed her to the door and down the hall toward the Lorans suite.

"There was one in our place, too," she said lowly. "Pete broke it with one of his ball bearings. It would be too much of a good thing if we broke the one in your suite as well."

He grunted concern. "I don't like this. Rooms bugged already. You think they suspect us?"

She shrugged tiny shoulders. They were proceeding down the hall, hand in hand, a pretty picture of an oversized man and a trusting child. She said, "They probably keep a twenty-four hour watch on every alien on Falange. They didn't particularly pick on us."

He growled, "That'll probably mean we'll have tails, too. Restrict our movements."

They reached the door of the Lorans suite and entered.

Helen told him where Pierre and Martha had gone and he thought about it awhile nodding acceptance. "It'll probably come to nothing, but I'll admit I can't think of anything else either." He walked over to the window and stared out, and she joined him, standing at his side, her head barely high enough to see over the sill.

She said, with unwonted softness, "It's not an unattractive city, Dorn. It's, well, something like a Tri-Di historical set."

He said, "It looks like prints I've seen of Nineteenth century Madrid. See that area down there? It's almost a replica of the Plaza Mayor."

"It's beautiful," she said.

79

"Yes, perhaps. The original Plaza Mayor is where the Inquisition held its famed *autos de fé*. I wonder what the equivalent is here."

She looked up at him, an element of exasperation there. "Does there have to be an equivalent?"

"I'm afraid there does. For centuries this culture hasn't moved an iota, either up or down. It's not a natural trait in civilized man. There's only one answer. When someone attempts to move it, he's clobbered. They've built up an efficient machine to do the clobbering. It was no mistake that the *Policia Secreta* detected our first three agents and eliminated them. Section G operatives are supposedly the most effective in United Planets but thus far it's been unable to make a dent in this throwback society."

She sighed. "But it's still a beautiful city, something like a museum."

Dorn Horsten grunted and his eyes went up to the sky. "Out there," he said, "are the alien worlds. Frighteningly near. Sooner or later, man will be face-to-face with that alien race. As things stand now, we know only that they are megayears in advance of us. The longer we can put off the confrontation, the better, but it is a matter of time."

"I know, I know. And we can't afford anachronisms such as Falange. It is later than we think."

He turned back to the room. "What did you have in mind, if and when we are able to locate the trial papers pertaining to our subversive colleague?"

Helen plopped herself into a chair and frowned prettily. "We didn't take in any further than that. Damn it, I wish I'd got Pierre to order some cognac before they went off. I could use another drink."

SECTION G: UNITED PLANETS

At the dinner table in the hotel restaurant that evening, Pierre Lorans stared down at the soup plate the waiter had put before him.

He demanded, "What is that?"

The waiter said anxiously, "It is *gazpacho,* Senor Lorans. The chef is awaiting your verdict."

"Then," Lorans said ominously, "he will wait until Mercury freezes over."

Martha said, "Now, Pierre."

Helen giggled.

Lorans ignored his family and held up the fingers of his left hand to enumerate for the squirming waiter. He ticked them off with his right hand, as he lectured.

"*Gazpacho* is without doubt the most superlative cold soup ever devised. It is basically oil and vinegar, but it is not *gazpacho* until finely strained tomatoes, garlic, bread crumbs, chopped cucumber, green pepper, and sometimes onions, are added. I myself am not strongly opinionated on the matter of the onions; over the years I have vacillated. Immediately before serving the *gazpacho,* croutons are added."

The waiter squirmed, his eyes went around the dining room. Those at the nearest tables were listening in. Lorans was making no attempt to keep his voice low.

"Yes, Senor Lorans," the waiter said. And he made the mistake of repeating, "The chef is anxious to have your valuable opinion."

"My opinion is that he is an idiot," Lorans said flatly. "Where, in the name of the Holy Ultimate. are the cucumbers?"

"Cucumbers?" The waiter closed his eyes in suffering and said, "I do not know what these cucumbers are."

Lorans took a deep breath, as though restraining himself. "I am sure you don't. Please take this swill away. No eels on this foreaken planet, no dried cod, and now no cucumbers! Away with it. Away!"

The waiter took up the plate of chilled soup and began to return in the direction of the kitchen.

Lorans said imperiously, "And that of my wife and daughter as well. I refuse to allow them to eat swill."

"Now, Pierre," Martha said. "It isn't as bad as all that. I tasted it."

"Silence. I insist. No swill."

Helen giggled. "I don't like soup anyways," she tinkled. She evidently spotted Doctor Dorn Horsten for the first time. He was seated at a table on the other side of the room.

Helen waved at him. "Uncle Dorn! Uncle Dorn!"

It seemed to all but break his face, but he managed a stolid smile and a slight wave in return. He was evidently nearly through his own meal.

The Lorans table maintained a chilly quiet while awaiting the next course. Even the exuberant Helen seemed frozen to silence by her father's irritation.

When the waiter returned, he was accompanied by the head waiter, who hovered about while his underling served the new dish.

"And what is this?" Pierre Lorans demanded.

The headwaiter bowed. "The Posada's speciality, Senor Lorans. *Pastel de Pescado.*"

"Fish pie, eh? Then you do have fish, at least of sorts, on this forsaken world?"

The headwaiter was suave. "Yes, Senor Lorans, If I am not mistaken, the white fish utilized by the chef in *Pastel de Pescado* is remarkably similar to the sole of Mother Earth."

Pierre Lorans touched the plate the waiter had put before him and seemed somewhat mollified when he found it so hot as to be almost untouchable.

He waited until the others had been served and then cautiously tasted. The headwaiter and waiter both held their breaths. Lorans tasted again.

Martha and Helen were eating rapidly, as though they had been through this before and knew what was coming.

Pierre Lorans, his face expressionless, put down his fork. He said to the headwaiter, "I am willing to give the chef the benefit of the doubt. Everybody has a bad day. Undoubtedly, it is a bad day. Perhaps he is seriously ill . . . probably on the verge of death. Martha! Helen!"

He came to his feet.

Martha and Helen, both with a sigh, put down their own utensils and stood also.

The headwaiter wrung his hands, his Iberian face in agony.

Lorans said, "We shall resort to our emergency supplies." He turned and stalked toward the door, followed by Martha, apology all over her face, with the rear brought up by Helen who had snagged a hard roll from the table before leaving.

All eyes followed the celebrated chef. Half the guests looked down into their dishes, suspiciously, which was not missed by the headwaiter, who once again closed his eyes in agony. It had taken over ten years to build up the reputation of the restaurant as the best in New Madrid.

Pierre Lorans halted at the table of Doctor Horsten. He stared down at the dessert the other was about to take on with a spoon. "Is that supposed to be Spanish flan?" he said, and then tightened his plump lips while waiting for the answer.

The doctor looked a bit startled. "Why, I believe so." He looked at the menu. "Yes, flan."

Pierre Lorans puffed out his cheeks before saying, "My dear Doctor, it will poison you. I am convinced. Do me the honor to adjourn to our rooms with us. I have been through this before. We never travel without our emergency supplies. Among other items I have a few tins of Camembert. Real Camembert from Normandy. I have also a bottle or two of stoneage Martell cognac. You can finish your, ah, meal with us. Camembert, rather than pseudo-flan. While we make do as best we can."

"Why . . . why . . ." the doctor hesitated

Behind her husband, Martha was nodding emphatically for the other to accept the invitation. On the face of it, she didn't want to be alone with her enraged spouse.

"Very well, very gracious of you, I am sure," Dorn Horsten said, putting down his napkin and coming to his feet. "Very old Martell, eh? Imagine that. It's been years. Actually real cognac, not the synthetic?"

Pierre Lorans looked at him, his lips beginning to go pale.

The doctor coughed his throat clear. "Ummm, yes, of course. It wouldn't . . . ah, couldn't be anything else but genuine cognac," he said.

Lorans turned on his heel again and marched out, followed by Martha, then Doctor Horsten, with Helen bringing up the rear. She managed to snag another roll from the doctor's table as she passed. Obviously, Helen was an old hand at this particular type of emergency.

In the Lorans suite, Pierre Lorans darted a look up at the bug he had smashed earlier. He looked at Helen, then Dorn Horsten, even as he was talking at full pitch about something involving eels, codfish and cucumbers.

Helen hissed, "Allez Oop!"

The hulking doctor grabbed her about the waist and tossed her aloft. Her head all but touched the ceiling, a chubby hand went out and, briefly, grasped the chain that held the chandelier; she seemed to be poised in the air.

She said, "It hasn't been repaired," twisted her body and fell gracefully into the arms of the big man beneath.

Lorans, still mouthing his rage and dwelling upon the alleged inedible fish pie he had been served, darted a look at his watch.

"All right," he whispered. "Fifteen minutes." Then he went back to his loud monologue which most certainly could have been heard through the suite's door to the hall.

Dorn Horsten went over to the window, flung it open and vaulted out.

Martha winced. "I'll never get used to seeing him do things like that," she said.

Helen jumped up to the window sill and peered down. "It's only four floors," she said. "Besides, there's a lawn down there. After all, he comes from a high gravity planet. Bye, bye."

And with that she launched herself after Horsten.

Martha winced again.

Down below, the doctor caught his diminuitive partner neatly and they started hurrying their way through the small park that edged the Posada San Francisco on this side. He didn't bother to put her down. Her small legs weren't up to the pace. Instead, she perched on his right shoulder.

He said, "How in the name of Holy Jumping Zen did Pierre and Martha locate this place? Sheer luck?"

· "Evidently, it couldn't have been easier," Helen told him. "They took a tour of the city, and one of the first things the guide pointed out was the *Policia Secreta* headquarters. Pete and Martha were suitably impressed and the flunky blabbered out just about everything they wanted, without their more than barely guiding his conversation. They asked why it was necessary to have such a large police, and he told them all about the subversives who had recently been caught. Standing there in the street, he pointed out the window of the room where interrogations were alleged to take place. Then he pointed out a window which was the only one, evidently, that opened onto the room where the vaults in which the archives are kept. Oh, he was most helpful."

The doctor grunted. He was walking at a rapid pace now, the girl on his shoulder. A passerby would probably have smiled at the pleasant picture they made. However, there were no other pedestrians at this hour. The Falangists supped late and went almost immediately to bed afterwards.

"I hope we find what we're looking for," he said. "But I doubt it. You brought that supposed toy of yours, didn't you? The rings that actually connect into a set of knuckledusters?"

"You think I'm stupid, you big lummox? Of course I brought them."

"No," Dorn Horsten sighed. "I don't think you're stupid. But I'm certainly glad you're the size you are."

"Why?" she said suspiciously.

"Because if you were my size, I might ask you to marry me, and the very thought changes my muscles to water."

"Why, you overgrown oaf."

86

"That must be it, up ahead," he said. "No other build-ing would be quite so large and quite so grim looking. Now, let me remember how Martha told me to locate that window."

They found the spot from which the Lorans had ob-served the building earlier.

Helen said, "You think there's a guard there?"

"Evidently. It's one of the few windows in the building with a light. This whole wing is dark except for it." He sized up the situation. "I hope they didn't repair the win-dow as yet."

Helen was on the ground now, chubby fists on her hips. "Not in this country. One of the things they brought from Mother Earth most enthusiastically was the do-it-Manana philosophy. I've already noticed that. How in the world did Pete manage to break it, anyway?"

Horsten was still casing the situation. He said absently, "You know him. He simply waited until nobody else was around, and then, while Martha distracted the guide's attention, he reached down, picked up a half brick or some other stone, and heaved it. Evidently, a few min-utes later a couple of *Guardia Civil* came dashing from the building, but they didn't even bother to question the Lorans. The guide was mystified by their questions. When they pointed out the window, high above, the guide said reasonably that nobody could throw a brick that high, and, anyway, they hadn't seen any young people, or any criminal types loitering in the vicinity."

Dorn Horsten came to a decision. He said, "I think I can make it up that wall. The gravity of this planet seems to be a mite less than even Mother Earth's and that brickwork will give hand and toe holds. However, I can't go into that window and get down into the room beyond

87

if there's an armed guard there. He'd zap me before I could get to him."

"Funker," Helen sneered. "Put all the strongarm stuff onto a little girl."

"All right, all right," he said. "Got any better ideas?"

"No," she said. And then, "Allez Oop!"

He swung the miniature gymnast and acrobat around several times before releasing her. She sailed in an impossible flight to the iron bars that sheltered the window. A tiny hand shot out and grasped them.

There was ample room to squeeze her childish body through. She paused a moment there, turned and made an age-old gesture to the man below, a circle with thumb and forefinger. He lumbered quickly to the wall and started scrambling up, hand over hand. He could see her tiny body swing through and cursed beneath his breath that she had gone on ahead before he arrived on the scene.

He reached the window and, supporting himself with one hand, tore the iron bars off with the other. He knocked what was left of the glass out of the way and squeezed through, though with some difficulty. He then dropped to the floor below.

Helen stood there, absently shining the brass knucks on her chubby right hand with the palm of her left. She said, her voice at its most childish treble, "Where've you been so long, you slow moving cloddy?"

He stared about the room. It was obviously devoted to special records. A sort of file within files arrangement. He looked down at the uniformed man who was stretched out on the floor.

"What did you do to him," he said.

"Nothing much," Helen said modestly. "He was somewhat startled to see me dropping out of the heavens. He was able to cross himself exactly once before I slugged him."

Horsten grunted. "What I wanted to know was, will he revive fairly soon?" He squatted next to the Falangist guard and slapped his face back and forth stingingly.

"Easy," Helen said. "You'll break his jaw."

The guard's eyes opened and at first expressed disbelief and then suddenly widened into terror. He reached clumsily for his side arm.

Horsten took it gently from his hand. It was a long-barreled 9mm military pistol of a period so remote that on Earth it would have taken its place in a museum. Horsten bent the barrel and made a knot in it and handed it back.

He said to the guard, most gently, "Where are the records of the subversion trial of the Earthling?"

The other was bug-eyeing the gun.

Horsten said, "Please, Senor, you would not want me to have to. . . ." He let the sentence dribble away.

The guard said, "No. No, no. I do not know what you want. But it is impossible."

"What's impossible?"

"I do not have the combination"

Horsten took the gun back again and bent the barrel into a sort of pretzel shape, to the other's horrified fascination.

"I didn't ask you that, did I?" Horsten said in kindly voice.

The guard pointed weakly at a large, iron safe. "Those are the top secret files pertaining to attempts to overthrow the government of the Caudillo."

Horsten came to his feet and looked down at the other

contemplatively. Helen had been scouting the room, now she took her place beside him.

"We should crisp him," the scientist muttered.

She took a deep breath and held her elbows tightly against her sides, in feminine rejection.

He looked at her in disgust. "All right, all right, I haven't got the guts either." He bent quickly and seemingly tapped the fallen man across the jawbone almost affectionately. His eyes rolled upward.

Horsten growled. "Look around for some wire, or rope, anything to tie him with."

"An old-fashioned telephone over here," she said.

The doctor went over and ripped it out and returned to tie the guard.

Moments later, that worthy revived enough, once more, to see his assailants leaving. The man with the 600 pound safe under one arm, the little girl seated on a shoulder.

She saw his eyes open and waved, "Goo' bye, Mr. Policeman."

He closed his eyes again and started in on several prayers he had not got around to using since childhood, and then and there swore off drinking anis after dinner.

XI

When Derek Lamb landed from the space shuttle craft, at the Stalingrad spaceport, it was to be received by a delegation backed by a forty piece band and a couple of hundred infantrymen at attention. The band was playing *The Internationale,* but Derek Lamb didn't know that. He had never heard *The Internationale* before, and for his taste he could wait a long time before he heard it again. In his time, on various words, he had heard blared *God Save the King, Deutschland uber Alles,* the *Star Spangled Banner,* and the *Marseilles,* and, not being a nationalist himself, they'd all sounded on the ridiculous side to him. For Derek Lamb, as all other agents of Section G, you could stick nationalism where it would create the most pain, anatomically speaking.

The delegation largely seemed thrown from the same mold that had produced Major Kulski, that is, they didn't seem especially impressive intellectually. The major introduced Derek around, and Derek did his best to try and remember the identities, not knowing to what extent he might be running into these people later.

Introductions over—the band playing the *Red Flag,* another piece Derek didn't recognize—all filed over to where a bevy of black limousines awaited. The Section G man was somewhat surprised to see that the vehicles were wheeled rather than aircushioned. In this field, at least, the Stalinists were behind the more advanced planets technologically.

The major and he rode in the second limousine, which was chauffeur-driven, an indication to the Section G agent that the roads were not automated. In this day and age, on a supposedly industrialized planet? Derek ran a thoughtful forefinger over his upper front teeth. Very interesting.

The spaceport was some twenty kilometers out of the city of Stalingrad. Derek kept his eyes open on the way in. By Mother Earth standards and those of the other more advanced worlds, agriculture was primitive, almost completely unautomated, and the fields worked by men and women, personally present. This was getting more ridiculous by the minute. One expected these things to take place on such worlds as Nature and the anarchist planet Kropotkin, where they deliberately foreswore industrialization, but Stalin, with its communist system, supposedly doted on it. He wondered what was expected to be accomplished. They could have imported the needed technics from Mother Earth, or many of the other United Planets worlds.

They sped through the streets and he noted the sparseness of vehicular traffic, the uniform drabness of the houses and other buildings, the colorlessness of the clothing of most of the pedestrians. One hardly got the impression of prosperity. Lack of prosperity on an industrialized world?

The caravan debouched into a huge square to one side of which was what Derek Lamb assumed to be a large fortress, certainly an anachronism beyond belief.

What good was a fortress in view of the weapons which prevailed in those parts of United Planets which maintained them at all? He didn't know it, but he was seeing a replica of the Kremlin and Red Square, copied as accurately as possible. They sped around the north of the fortress, to a monstrous iron gate, guarded by a squad of six infantrymen armed with rifles. They sprang to the salute, the gate swung open, and the convoy of cars, going only slightly slower than before, sped up a curving, cobblestoned ramp.

Inside, the area seemed even larger than it had from without. Derek couldn't know it, but the Kremlin, in the early days of Russia, had been the whole city of Moscow.

They pulled up before a large, three story building of white granite. Had such a building been on Mother Earth, the Section G man decided, it would have been converted into a museum. Surely it must have been copied architecturally from some edifice of possibly the Sixteenth Century, if not older.

The major said, "This is the *Bolshoi Kremlevski Dvorets,* the Great Kremlin Palace, in Earth-Basic language. It is our destination. The Chairman of the Presidium resides here and also maintains his offices."

"Excellent," Derek said.

They got out of their vehicle and approached the large doors of carved wood. None of the occupants of the other limousines accompanied them. There were two guards, who presented arms at their approach. It would seem that the major was both known and expected. No identification was requested. The doors swung open.

Inside they were confronted with the most garishly ornate hall Derek Lamb could ever remember having

93

seen. He thought of the atmosphere as Victorian with its crystal chandeliers, its impossibly hideous and uncomfortable chairs, its life-size statuary, its antiquated Socialist Realism school paintings, and its broad staircase of marble.

They mounted the stairway, turned left down a corridor that was in as bad taste as the hall below.

They walked perhaps a hundred feet before coming to a massive door of inlaid bronze. Two more guards were stationed here, both of officer rank, both armed with side arms, rather than rifles. They saluted, and this time Major Kulski returned it. One of them hastened to open the door.

Inside was a reception room, with two desks flanking another bronze door. At the desk were two more junior officers. They looked up at the entrance of the major and his charge.

Major Kulski said, "Colonel Inspector Ilya Simonov of the planet Lenin, on appointment to see Comrade Alex Vavilov, Chairman of the Presidium of the Central Committee."

The two officers could have been twins. Both were blond, both blue-eyed, both about six feet, about one hundred and sixty-five, both nattily uniformed, and both very sharp of eye. They were the two most impressive Stalinists that Derek had seen thus far.

One of them said to the major, "He has been searched, of course?"

"Yes, on the satellite. With every detection device at our command. Every article in his possession has been gone over and over again. Not a single suspicious item."

"Very well." The other came to his feet. He looked

Derek in the face, obviously summing him up. "I am Captain Leonid Leonov, aide to the Chairman. Please follow me, Comrade Colonel." He turned and led the way. Major Kulski began to come along as well, but Captain Leonov said, "Your presence will not be required, Major. You will wait here."

The major seemed somewhat surprised, but his not to question why, of course. He reversed his engines and took an uncomfortable looking chair. Evidently, an aide to the Chairman, even though only a captain, ranked an ordinary major.

The room beyond the bronze door was possibly the largest office Derek had ever seen. It was also the most ornate and for his money uncomfortable. A one quarter acre desk sat in its exact center, a smaller desk to one side.

Behind the larger desk sat a small man who was as near to the exact opposite of what Derek had expected Alex Vavilov, dictator of the planet Stalin, to be as possible. Had he been much shorter, he would have been pushing midget class. He was on the thinnish side, except for his belly which was like a good-sized round watermelon. His face was pinched and suspicious, his eyes were dull and watery. He was the most ridiculous caricature of the chief of a power elite the Section G man could imagine. It was all Derek could do to keep from gaping at him.

The captain said formally, "Chairman Vavilov, may I present Colonel Inspector Ilya Simonov, of the planet Lenin?"

The dictator nodded and ran his rheumy, suspicious eyes over Derek, who was standing at attention.

95

He said finally, in a thin, unsteady voice which went well with his unprepossessing physical appearance, "Well . . . well, sit down, uh, confound it. Sit down."

Derek Lamb took a chair across from the desk and Captain Leonov sat at the smaller desk.

Vavilov said, "Well . . . well . . . what is this confounded secret message from Vladimir Mazurov, my equal number of the planet Lenin? Confound it, I've never even heard of the planet Lenin. Captain, have you ever heard of the planet Lenin?"

Captain Leonov said smoothly, "Chairman Vavilov, I understand that it is on the far side of the United Planets confederation. Undoubtedly, it has as little communication with other worlds as do we ourselves."

Derek Lamb looked at the captain. This was a sharp one. He had avoided revealing that he, also, had never heard of Lenin, beyond the false information in Derek's passport.

Derek said to the Presidium Chairman, "Comrade Vavilov, my words are for your ears alone, according to my orders. At least, at this stage of the game."

"What . . . what, confound it? Here you are. Speak . . . uh, up. Speak up."

Derek said carefully, "The captain?"

The captain's eyes smiled.

Vavilov said, "Nonsense . . . sheer nonsense. The captain is my aide. There is nothing you can say to me that he cannot hear. This is all confounded nonsense." The Chairman scratched his rounded tummy in irritation.

Captain Leonov said smoothly, "I am the Chairman's bodyguard as well as his aide, Comrade Colonel Inspector."

"I see," Derek said. "Very well." He took a deep

breath. "Comradely greetings from the Presidium of the Central Committee of Lenin and from Chairman Mazurov. As you undoubtedly know, Lenin was settled almost identically as was Stalin. Our institutions are the same as your own admired ones. We strive only to preserve the Revolution."

Vavilov listened to that impatiently. He said to the captain, "Leonid, some vodka."

Derek held his peace while Captain Leonid Leonov came to his feet, went over to what seemed a bookcase and touched a button. A section of the bookcase slid away to reveal a very complete bar. He opened the refrigerator, brought forth a well chilled bottle, took up three large shot glasses and returned with them to his superior's desk. He filled the glasses carefully, served his superior first, then Derek, took his own glass and returned to his desk.

This time, there was no toast. The dictator stiff-wristed the spirits back ·down his gullet, with an elan beyond his physical appearance. The other two dutifully followed suit.

"Well . . . well . . . go on. What is your message?"

"Comrade, it consists of two parts. First, as you undoubtedly know, we are not members of United Planets, although you of Stalin have taken that step. Chairman Mazurov seeks your opinion on the desirability of our joining."

The inadequate-looking dictator peered at him through dull eyes. "Is that all of this secret message which is so important?"

"No, Comrade."

The captain had chuckled softly.

"Well . . . well, what's the rest of it?"

Derek said deliberately, "Comrade Chairman, our institutions are almost identical. Our problems then, must be similar. On Lenin there is a considerable movement to overthrow the Revolution. If this can happen on our world, it can happen on yours. My superiors suggest we unite and cooperate in suppressing such counter revolution."

The captain said smoothly, "But there is no counter revolution on Stalin, Comrade Colonel. All is tranquil. The people are happy under the benevolent guidance of the Chairman and the Central Committee of the Party."

"Yes . . . yes, confound it, of course," Vavilov muttered. He took up the vodka bottle and poured again. "But what did your Chairman have in mind?"

"Exchanging methods, exchanging viewpoints on how to combat the counter revolution," Derek said, tossing down his fresh drink. "Even though perhaps you have no such problem today, perhaps its ugly reactionary, imperialist head will rear itself sometime in the future. We should cooperate."

"In which manner would this cooperation manifest itself at this time?" the captain said softly.

Derek took him in. It was obvious that the other was a goddamned smarter character than his ultimate superior. He said, "At this stage, it was thought desirable for me to investigate your methods to the fullest. To find out how you handle police matters, and how you combat sabotage, subversion and counter revolution. I was to spend as much time as necessary here, and then return to report to Lenin. Further negotiations could then be entered into between us."

"Well . . . well, confound it," Vavilov said, pouring

still another dosage of vodka for the three of them. "What do you think, Leonid?"

But the captain didn't have a chance to answer that. A small red light flashed on his desk.

He said to Derek, "Pardon me, Comrade. A priority signal." He flicked a switch and put on a headset.

He listened for several minutes and then took off the headset. He put it down carefully on his desk and looked at Derek thoughtfully.

The Chairman said, "Well . . . well, confound it."

Captain Leonid Leonov said slowly, "Chairman Vavilov, the signal was a tight beam from our embassy on Mother Earth. They have been checking there. It seems that there is no such planet as Lenin."

XII

Ross Metaxa said, "Did Ronny Bronston say anything else?"

"Yes," Li Chang Chu said. "The rest of the message was, 'Me make big talk . . . No more Number One.' "

Sid Jakes, who had been sitting erect in unwonted fashion, said excitedly, "He's going to address the whole planet. All of Doria. Make some sort of announcement. Free elections, after his abdication, or something."

"Impossible," Metaxa rumbled. "Fantastic." He glared at Li Chang. "How do you know it was really Ronny?"

"Who else on Doria would know Mandarin, or, even if they did, know enough to beam a message to Section G in that tongue?"

"Kidnap El Primero." Sid Jakes said in second thought. "What kind of drivel-happy curd is that? We all know he's the most security conscious dictator in United Planets. How could you ever kidnap the funker, not to speak of substituting someone in his place?"

Li Chang looked at him strangely and spoke hesitantly, as though she hated to say the words. "I can think of only one possibility. According to our dossier on Michael Ortega, he has one Achilles' heel. Remember Svetlana Alliluyeva? Or, better, Svetlana Stalin?"

Sid Jakes bothered to shake his head. Ross Metaxa merely poured himself another drink of Denebian tequila and waited for her to go on.

"The only person Josef Stalin evidently really cared for," Li Chang said. "His daughter and one of the very few relatives, friends and associates that long survived him. Well, from what I hear, Michael Ortega has the equivalent in Concha Ortega."

Metaxa growled, "What's this got to do with Bronston and his taking over the position of El Primero?"

Li Chang made a feminine gesture with her slight shoulders. "It wouldn't be the first time our quiet, unassuming Ronald has made his mark with the ladies. Remember Amazonia?"

Sid laughed suddenly. "So one of our teams tried to bribe El Primero's guards. The second troupe tried to blow him up from a distance. But Ronny turns on the Bronston charm and—" Sid Jakes ground to a halt. "Holy Jumping Zen," he yelped. "Sam Goodboy. He'll be gunning for Ronny!"

Ross Metaxa spun in his chair and blurted into his orderbox, "Irene! Sam Goodboy, a new agent. On assignment to Doria. What's his cover?"

Li Chang and Sid Jakes failed to make out the answer.

Metaxa snapped, "Find out, soonest. A mistake has been made. He's on assignment to kill Ronny Bronston."

"And . . . he . . . never . . . fails" Li Chang added, her voice so low as hardly to be made out.

"And he never fails," Metaxa repeated into the interoffice communicator.

For a moment, Irene Kasansky held silence, then she said, the usual rasp gone from her voice, "I didn't handle Goodboy's cover. I'll check immediately."

SECTION G: UNITED PLANETS

Metaxa looked back at his two top supervisors.

"He never fails?" he questioned sourly. "Anybody can fail, no matter how proficient. Certainly, professional killers can."

Li Chang was shaking her head. "Ross . . . this one doesn't use weapons. He's one of my Special Talent recruits."

Her superior looked at her in puzzlement. "You mean judo or one of those other old——"

She was still shaking her head. "He doesn't know how he does it." She added, as though that explained everything, "He comes from the planet Rubata."

"Rubata!" Jakes snorted. "Those crackpots."

She turned to him, frowning again. "If you will." She went back to Metaxa. "You'll recall the planet was originally colonized by would-be witches, spiritualists, psi adepts, or would-be adepts, so forth and so on."

"Vaguely," Metaxa growled. "As Sid said, crackpots." He took down his drink.

Li Chang shrugged prettily. "I would have said the same, until I began my search for special talents to recruit for Section G. Quite a few of them have come from Rubata. Few would deny that down through the ages the human race has produced some, well, out of the ordinary persons. Do you deny, for instance, that ocasionally a human turns up with total recall? That others have the ability to do mathematical problems in their heads that put computers to shame? I won't mention such recorded phenomenon as telepathy, clairvoyance and even precognition. However, we have several Special Talents agents who can exercise any of these to a greater or lesser extent."

"All right." Metaxa muttered in irritation. "So from

time to time offbeat talents have shown. I'll accept that, in a limited way. What's it got to do with this Sam Goodboy?"

"The original colonists of Rubata numbered but a few thousand," Li Chang pursued. "However, they bred—with each other, obviously." She shrugged again. "Not only did the posterity continue and strengthen those, you might say, offbeat talents, but evolved some new ones. Among the original colonists were witch doctors, and libans, sorcerers and wizards, hex doctors and shamanists, practitioners of black magic, of voodoo, of the left hand path . . . admittedly, as Sid has put it, largely crackpots. But you can't explain away, with that term alone, all the evidence that has come down to us through the ages of such items as bantu witchmen, voodoo priests and hex doctors killing persons through their . . . special talents. At any rate, Sam Goodboy's own belief is that he numbers at least several of these among his ancestors, not to speak of telepaths, clairvoyants and so forth. The thing is, this talent of his *works*."

The orderbox spoke up. Irene. said, "Commissioner, I've tracked down Goodboy's cover. He's going in as a tourist. Doria makes a play for tourism. It is supposed to be very scenic and they evidently can use the interplanetary credits."

Metaxa said, "All right, all right. How's he getting there? We'll have to contact him on his ship."

"He's on the Space Passenger-Freighter *Mola*." She hesitated, then added. "Commissioner, it's under Dorian registry."

"That doesn't make any difference. We'll contact him in our own code."

Li Chang said emptily, "He isn't checked out on Section G code, Ross. Even if he was, Dorian security is familiar with our codes. Remember, they number two of our former troupes in their secret police."

Sid Jakes was on his feet. He bent over the orderbox. "Irene," he said. "Get a move on. Arrangements for Supervisor Chu and myself to depart soonest for Doria. If necessary, requisition a Space Forces four-manner."

Rex Metaxa scowled at him. "We can't risk your neck on a drivel-happy romp like this."

Jakes looked at him bleakly. "Ronny Bronston is my best field man, Ross. On top of that, Doria is one of the biggest sore thumbs in United Planets right now. If that planet spills all it knows about the inner workings of Section G, then the member planets will begin dropping out of the confederation like hail." ·

Li Chang was standing as well. "I'll get ready," she said.

XIII

Colonel Miguel Segura looked about the room unbelievingly. His eyes finally came back to the *Guardia Civil* private. He said, "The story again?"

"Senor Colonel, I do not know how many of them there were, nor even where they came from. I was here, wide awake. Suddenly, they were upon me. There must have been at least six."

One of the colonel's assistants said, "I would think so, if they managed to get that safe out of here and all the way down and out of the building."

The colonel rasped, "Quiet, Raul. Go on with the story."

"I fought as best I could. There were too many. They beat me unconscious and tied me. When I awoke, the safe was gone. That is all I know."

The colonel looked at the other unbelievingly and uncomprehendingly. He pointed at the broken window above. "The bars are broken from that window. Why? How? Surely they couldn't have done that without you hearing. But even if they could have, why? The safe was too large to have been let out there."

"Senor Colonel," the guard told him. "I do not know. It is all as though the work of devils."

The colonel sighed deeply. "If it were not for the fact that the safe has been found, the door torn off, in the park, I could hardly credit a word of this."

Another aide came in. The Colonel looked at him in irritation. "Yes?"

The newcomer said, "The clerks have been through the papers contained in the safe. There are only a very few missing."

"Well?"

"They pertained to the recent trial of the suspected Section G agent and his accomplices."

The colonel shook his head and returned his stare to the guard. "Where did you say they came from? Supposedly the door was locked from the inside, but you say they burst suddenly upon you."

The subject of interrogation squirmed. "Senor Colonel, I do not know. Uhhh, it was as though they descended from the heavens."

Colonel Miguel Segura—chief inspector of the Neuvo Madrid *Policia Secreta* and rumored to be one of the handful of men who spent their evenings with El Caudillo playing cards, sipping spirits imported from Mother Earth, and being entertained by flamenco dancers—had sent his card in formally.

He was in full uniform and accompanied only by his youthful aide, Teniente Raul Dobarganes, also in formal attire. Their manner was grave and, if anything, overly polite.

Doctor Horsten had been located and brought to the Lorans suite so that all could be addressed at once. They were seated, save Helen, who stood, toes pointed in, hands clasped behind her back, and staring up at Teniente Dobarganes, unblinkingly. It had to be admitted, the dress uniform of the *Policia Secreta* was not exactly drab.

The two police officers had hardly finished their formal bows than Pierre Lorans shot to his feet dramatically. He crossed his arms over his chest. "I confess," he blurted. "I admit everything."

Inspector Segura stared at him. "You do?"

"Yes! Everything! I should never have come to this barbarian planet. Police everywhere. No freedom for the artist, such as myself. I should have known better. It is impossible for me to equivocate. Impossible. I am a Nouveau Cordon Bleu chef. I am willing to die rather than give up my principles."

He shut his mouth and stood there defiantly.

Martha began to cry.

Helen didn't even bother to turn. She continued to stare up at the lieutenant, stationed no more than three feet from him.

The Doctor looked blank.

The Inspector raised eyebrows to his assistant, who shrugged a shrug that would have done every Spaniard since the Phoenicians first came to trade for tin, full proud.

The Colonel turned his eyes back to the defiant chef. "And just what is it that you confess?" he said cautiously.

"To insulting this benighted, probably starving planet! Its food, its chefs, its lack of even such simplicities as *bacalao,* eels, cucumbers. It's. . . ."

The Colonel held up a hand to stem the tide.

"Please, Senor Lorans, will you be seated? This is a very serious matter."

107

The lips of Senor Lorans began to go pale.

Martha said hurriedly, "Now, Pierre, please sit down. You are not being insulted. We must at least hear what Sergeant What's-his-name wants. And nobody is arresting you, Pierre."

The Colonel shot a look from the side of his eyes, upon her calling him a sergeant, but the face of Raul Dobarganes was without expression.

When Lorans had been lured back into his chair, the Colonel took up again, though not without misgivings. He began, "Dear guests of Falange——"

Helen said, "I think you're pretty." But she was talking to Teniente Dobarganes, not the inspector, not even the mother of whom would have possibly considered the description.

Raul Dobarganes could feel the pink ascending from his tight collar.

"Gosh, you even blush pretty," Helen told him with considerable satisfaction.

Martha said, "Helen, you be quiet now. The gentlemen have something to say." She smiled sweetly, albeit somewhat condescendingly, at the Colonel. "You go right ahead, Sergeant."

Colonel Segura opened his mouth, closed it again. Paused for a long moment, then started all over.

He said to Pierre Lorans, "There is complete freedom on Falange, Senor. You have not observed correctly. This is the most stable socioeconomic system ever devised. All of our people are happy. All are in their place. Those whom the Holy Ultimate meant to administrate, do. Those whom fate meant to serve, serve. Everybody is satisfied with their lot on the planet Falange. Of how many of our sister members of United Planets can you say the same, eh?"

"Why, it sounds very nice," Martha nodded encouragingly.

Helen piped up. "Then how come you got so many cops everywheres?"

Both the colonel and his aide looked at her blankly for a long frustrated moment.

"Ah," Doctor Horsten murmured. "An interesting point. Out of the mouth of babes, so to speak." His stolid face took on an absentminded quality. "It seems to me I can think of a parallel some few centuries ago back on Mother Earth. A period during which the leading nations paraded about in great style loudly boasting of their degrees of freedom and how highly they valued peace and despised aggression. However, somehow, those who disclaimed loudest of their love of democracy, peace and freedom, had the largest police forces, secret police, intelligence agencies, armies and navies. Such nations as Switzerland and the Scandinavians, who didn't need to talk about their internal freedoms, invariably had small police forces and military, even judged on a per capita basis——"

The colonel interrupted, his voice snappish now, "Forgive me. Somehow we seem to have gotten off on a tangent. I must get to the point. Last night, a major crime was committed. One of such nature that only an alien could possibly be interested. You are some of the few aliens registered in this vicinity and, by coincidence, you arrived only yesterday, from Mother Earth, the planet involved."

"Mother Earth!" Pierre Loras blurted, unbelievingly. "Involved in a major crime?"

The inspector said dryly, "Rumors are beginning to

109

go through the member planets of United Planets that Mother Earth seems to have developed into a strange parent. However, the point is that you are within a quarter mile of the scene of the crime, and have just arrived from Earth."

Doctor Horsten said vaguely, "Crime. When did this, uh, crime take place, my dear Colonel?"

Segura said, "At almost exactly eleven o'clock."

The heavy-set scientist scowled and tried to remember. "I am afraid I have no, ah, what do they say on the crime tapes on Tri-Di? Alibi. Ah, yes. No albi."

The colonel looked at Raul Dobarganes who had at long last escaped the fascinated stare of little Helen. His assistant brought forth a report.

The colonel took it and said, "At eleven o'clock last night, Doctor, you were right here in this room. Senor Lorans had been dissatisfied with his evening meal and you all adjourned to this suite."

"Ha!" Lorans blurted and began to come to his feet. His wife restrained him.

"You are right," Doctor Horsten exclaimed. "I was right here with the Lorans family. A perfect alibi. I couldn't possibly have committed this terrible crime." A fascinated gleam came to his eyes behind their pince-nez glasses. "I love Tri-Di crime shows," he confided. "What happened last night? Mass murder? An armed romp? Perhaps——"

"Romp?" the colonel said blankly.

"A caper. A job! Perhaps they knocked off the National Treasury, huh?" Doctor Horsten came to his feet, portraying more excitement than anyone had ever expected this staid scientist to project. He held his hands

110

as though cradling a two-handed weapon. "Muffle guns," he said. "Come driving up in a fast hovercar. Leave a lookout outside. The rest go charging in, cutting down the guards. . . ."

The colonel, stricken to silence, had closed his eyes in the Iberian expression of agony the Section G operatives were beginning to get used to.

It was Dobarganes who took over. He put a hand on the excited Doctor's arm. "Please, Senor Horsten, it was not that at all. We never have that sort of crime on Falange. Please be seated." He got the good doctor into his chair and turned back to his superior. There was a strained element in his voice as well, by this time. "Senor Colonel?" he said.

The colonel had obviously decided to get it over with. He said, "The maids reported this morning that there was ash in your fireplace, as though papers had been burned there. It was, so far as we could analyze, paper of the type stolen last night. Undoubtedly, you have some explanation." He added, *sotto voce,* "Some weird explanation."

All except Helen looked blank. Helen was beginning to eye the colonel malevolently.

Martha said, "Why, why, I burned some papers last night. Heavens only knows why I ever brought them along when I packed."

"Senora, this paper was of the type stolen last night. Our laboratories. . . ."

Doctor Horsten had recovered from his enthusiasm. He grunted deprecation. "My   dear   dear   Colonel Sorghum——"

"Segura," Raul Dobarganes said quickly.

111

SECTION G: UNITED PLANETS

"I suspect your paper manufacturers produce various of the types originated by Mother Earth. Undoubtedly, Mrs. Lorans, among her other effects, brought an identical, or at least similar, paper along with her."

The colonel was scowling.

The scientist went on, a certain impatience in his voice now. "Otherwise, you could always put the Senora under, ah, what is the term they use on the crime shows? Scop. Yes, Scop, truth serum, eh? Surely you will be able to, ah, dig out of her the method by which she sneaked from this fourth floor suite down through the hotel, captured these documents, or whatever, smuggled them back and then burnt them to hide the crime." He turned his eyes to Martha. "My dear Mrs. Lorans, you have not seen enough Tri-Di spy tapes, the historic ones. You must chew up and swallow such secret papers."

Martha's face revealed that she didn't understand what either of them were talking about. And Pierre Lorans' face was just about as blank.

The colonel gave up. He was wondering why he had bothered to come here when any of a hundred underlings could have checked the remote lead. He began making his preliminary goodbyes toward leaving. However, he reckoned without Helen.

She had evidently come to her decision and advanced on the quick to give him a sharp kick in the shin. Startled, he bent to grab the leg assaulted.

She demanded in her childish treble, "What did you do to my Uncle Ferd? Did you go around arresting him too? Don't you hurt my Uncle Ferd."

The colonel looked appealingly at his aide who came forward hurriedly to the rescue, however, Helen had already been snatched up by her mother.

112

"Don't you dare arrest my Uncle Ferd!" Helen shrilled, hauled from the fray by Martha.

For a moment, the colonel thought he might have something. He snarled, "Who's Uncle Ferd?"

His lieutenant cleared his throat. "Probably the technician for the *corridas,* Senor Colonel. He arrived on the same spaceship, you'll recall. Senor Zogbaum."

"Oh, yes." The colonel straightened and did his gentlemanly best to smile at the child. "Your Uncle Ferd is very safe, little Senorita. He was in custody . . . ah, that is, he was guarded by friends all night, so he couldn't possibly be involved, uh, that is, couldn't be one of the gang of bad men. And now, Senora, Senores, little Senorita, forgive the Teniente and I for intruding upon you. *Hasta luego.*"

He and his aide got out more speedily than protocol usually called for on Falange, and once out in the hotel corridor, both wiped their foreheads with their handkerchiefs.

Back in the suite, Martha gestured upward at the bug.

Pierre Lorans took a pocketknife from his clothes and opened what would ordinarily have been the small blade, the end of which had been filed off to make a screwdriver. He handed it to Helen.

Helen said, "Allez oop," and in a moment duplicated her performance of the day before, poising for a long moment, partially supported by a tiny hand grasping the chandelier chain. The other hand darted out with the improvised screwdriver, loosening a screw slightly, then she fell over gracefully and back down into the arms of her partner.

Horsten tossed her high again, she gave the screw

another turn. On the third attempt, she pulled loose a wire before dropping away.

She muttered with satisfaction, "I'll bet whoever's in charge of bugging this suite is going slowly drivel-happy."

Back in chairs, they looked around at each other.

Horsten said to Martha, "You memorized the whole trial before burning it?"

"Of course."

"Why didn't you flush away *all* of the ashes?"

"Because to hide all signs of my burning some paper would have been practically impossible. By leaving a little ash, the fact of considerable burning was hidden. In that way, my story held up."

"I suppose so," Horsten said. "Some time today, Martha, it might be a good idea, while Pierre is busy with his colleague chefs, for you to go to the public library and memorize the Falange legal code. We might need it."

Helen said thoughtfully, "And while you're at it, all rules pertaining to the bullfights during this fantastic selection of their Caudillo."

"I think you're right," Martha said. "I'll do it."

Horsten looked at the plumpish Lorans. "At the rate you're going, they'll shoot you, or kick you off the planet, even before they find you're a Section G agent."

Lorans grinned one of his rare grins, which gave him an impish quality. "No. I'm impressing them more by the minute. They wouldn't dream of expelling such an obviously temperamental artist, until I have at least produced one complete repast. They recognize my type too well not to understand it. At this point, they're in awe. The present El Caudillo evidently considers himself a gourmet. Heads would roll if anything happened to me

114

before he could get his undoubtedly rounded belly under a table provided by my art."

Helen said, "The problem is, how do we get these two underground fellas out of the deep freeze?"

Martha looked at her. "Deep freeze?"

"That Alcazar political prison."

The doctor said unhappily, "And what do we do with them once we get out? We don't know where their friends may be, if they have any friends still at liberty. Very possibly they have no place to go to ground."

Helen said, "They can come here."

After their frigid reception of that, she snarled, "I'm not as simple as all that. Today, Pete goes out to buy some clothes suitable to Falange fashion. He buys several suits, including three that are semi-formal and very similar to the sort that the Posada waiters wear. Ready made—he hasn't time for tailoring. One suit will be slightly too large, one just right, one for a slimmer man. Most of these Falangists seem to average his size. Okay, we liberate the two former companions of our Section G agent who was shot as a subversive, bring them here and dress them in Pete's suits. We should be able to get some sort of fit.

"We keep them around the suite. If the police come in, they walk out, with trays, or towels, or whatever. Who ever looks at a hotel waiter?"

Lorans said sceptically, "Suppose a real waiter comes in?"

"There are four rooms, including the bath. We'll shuffle them around from room to room, in closets, under beds. Maybe we'll put over the idea that Martha doesn't like maids to make her bed, or even clean her room. She wants to do it herself. Hotels have more eccentric guests

115

than that. We can keep our refugees hidden in her room when the maids come in."

Lorans wiped a hand over his brow. "Talk about the Purloined Letter."

Horsten said, "It's a rather desperate measure."

Helen snapped, "All right, double-dome, think of something better."

Lorans said, "How are we going to get out of here to raid the prison? And, if we do, how will we locate them? What were their names, Martha?"

Martha said, "Bartolome Guerro and Jose Hoyos." She looked thoughtful. "I could probably find some sort of prison plan in the National Library."

"Hmmm," the doctor said. "I wonder if at the same time you could find a plan of the powerplant serving Neuvo Madrid."

Helen looked at him speculatively. "I don't trust you," she said.

Dorn Horsten beamed at her.

Colonel Segura, making his way by the beam of an old-fashioned flashlight, covered the small room thoroughly. He was beginning to doubt, these days, the reports of his own senses. The place was a shambles.

Finally, Raul Dobarganes bringing up the rear, the colonel returned to where two of his plainclothesmen had the hotel electrician pinned to a chair.

The colonel glowered down at that unfortunate. "You are under arrest," he snarled, "and will probably be shot for sabotage of government property. The Posada is operated by the *Policia Secreta* to keep an eye on aliens and other suspects, as you well know."

116

The electrician groaned and one of the plainclothes-men backhanded him across the mouth.

The colonel went on ominously. "You have one chance to save your miserable life. Tell us the purpose of your crime and reveal all accomplices."

The technician shook his head in mute denial and hopeless appeal for mercy.

The colonel, directing the beam of the electric torch full into the other's face, said, "Every light in the building has been extinguished and every device dependent on electricity is disrupted. Why! What did you expect to accomplish?"

The other moaned and the plainclothesman slapped him again.

The colonel sighed deeply. "Tell me your lie once again, traitor."

"I am not a traitor. I am no traitor——"

He achieved another stinging slap across the mouth.

"Senor Colonel, I swear by the United Temple, by the Holy Ultimate, it is exactly as I have told you. A strange, whirling something came in through the door. Even as it whirled, it moved, seemingly slowly, and in . . . in a half circle around the room. I was spellbound, hypno-tized. In all my life, Senor Colonel, I have never seen such a strange thing. I was paralyzed. It came in through the door, went down the room, whirling, whirling, and then came back and——"

"And hit you on the back of the head, you fool."

"Yes, Colonel," the other said in misery.

"And when you awoke. . . ."

"When I awoke, the control room was in a chaos. Everything capable of being smashed was smashed. It

117

could have been but a matter of minutes, but when I awoke there was damage of an extent that would have taken hours."

The colonel boiled inwardly and directed the beam of his flashlight upward. He said ominously, "There. That device, up near the ceiling, whatever it is. You can hardly see it from here. A group of saboteurs desiring to smash that would have had to have a ladder, a long ladder. Are you suggesting that they marched through the halls of this hotel carrying a ladder?"

"No, Senor Colonel," the other moaned. "I don't know——"

Another vicious slap.

The colonel snarled, "These whirling mysteries of yours are an attempt to hide the true facts, traitor. Something is going on here. You have accomplices. Several of them must have come here and joined with you to wreck your charge."

"No . . . no . . ."

Another *Policia Secreta* underling came hurrying into the room. Raul Dobarganes met him and spoke briefly in a low whisper, then approached his superior. The colonel looked up at him, impatiently.

Dobraganes said unhappily, "Senor Colonel, the electricity is now off all over the city. It is in darkness. Only the palace of El Caudillo, with its private power plant, has lights."

The colonel stared at him, as though his lieutenant was an idiot. "A temporary power break."

"No, Senor Colonel. From what this man says, there has been an unprecedented sabotage of the plant."

"Are you insane! There are a hundred guards!"

"Yes, Senor Colonel."

SECTION G: UNITED PLANETS

"Come along *Madre de Dios!* The world goes mad!" The colonel stormed for the door.

Behind him, the electrician sighed in relief and, as though in reflex, the plainclothesman smashed him across the mouth again.

XIV

The Chairman looked at Derek Lamb and at his aide stupidly. "No such planet?" he said.

"That is what Ambassador Gramatikov reports. He wished to send us as much basic information as he could find, but there is no such information in the United Planets data banks."

Derek cursed himself inwardly. He should have had Irene Kasansky fake such material and plant it in the data banks until his mission had been completed. This blew it.

One of the others must have pressed an alarm; the captain, undoubtedly, since his chief was obviously still so dumbfounded that he didn't know what was going on. At any rate, the room was suddenly full of armed soldiers, guns leveled at the Section G agent. They had materialized through two doors that had magically opened in the pseudo-bookshelves.

The Chairman was saying, "What . . . what . . . confound it."

Captain Leonid Leonov, who was eyeing Derek Lamb in amusement, said, "Comrade Vavilov, this man is an imposter. By Karl Marx himself, I haven't the vaguest idea of what his purpose might be. Your instructions, Comrade Vavilov?"

As Derek Lamb sat motionless, his mind racing without result, the Chief of State of Stalin tried to rise to the occasion. Vavilov's thin mouth worked.

He said finally, "Take him down to the cellars and put him to the question, Leonid. When you have found out everything, shoot him and report in full to me."

Captain Leonov must have pressed another button. The door to the outer room opened and the other aide entered, his face puzzled as soon as he saw the guards.

Leonid Leonov came to his feet, a heavy military pistol in hand. He said to Derek, with mock politeness, "This is Captain Nicholas Makeev, who will assist me in getting to the root of this matter." He turned to his colleague. "It seems as though the Colonel Inspector is an imposter. Comrade Chairman Vavilov has instructed us to put him to the question, down below, and then to, ah, shoot him."

The Chairman, still tittering his lack of comprehension of the whole thing, said, "Yes . . . yes, confound it. Shoot him and dispose of him in the usual manner. Shoot him."

Captain Makeev drew his own sidearm and scowled questioningly at Derek Lamb, who took a deep disgusted breath. Damn it, he should have been equipped with a cyanide pill. He had fouled this whole thing up to hell and gone. Now he was defenseless, couldn't even suicide.

Leonid Leonov said to Derek, "If you'll just come along, Colonel Inspector." He motioned with his gun to one of the doors through which the alert guards had burst.

Derek Lamb stood, shrugged, and headed for the door.

There was a remote possibility that he might be able to grab a gun from one of the others and shoot himself, but he doubted it.

He was correct. If nothing else, the two captains were fully efficient.

On the other side of the bookcase door, was a guard-room, and at its far side an elevator. The two captains, their eyes brightly alert, their guns ever at the ready, herded the Section G agent into it. Two of the guards came along.

The prison cellars were deep below the *Bolshoi Kremlevski Dvorets* and as he proceeded down the dank stone corridor, passing cell after cell, all of them seemingly empty, Derek Lamb had the damnedest feeling of being in one of the old horror shows which were sometimes revived on Tri-Di back on Mother Earth. Had a wolfman or vampire passed them, he wouldn't have been overly surprised.

They came to a steel door, heavily barred, and one of the guards went ahead and opened it. Inside was what would seem to be an operating room in a hospital. There was a white table in the center, various cabinets of instruments and what looked like medical supplies, about the walls. There was a slightly sinister aspect to the whole thing.

Captain Makeev said to the guards, "Station yourselves in the corridor. No one is to be allowed entrance. No one. Realize that Captain Leonov and I are acting under direct orders of the Chairman of the Presidium himself."

"Yes, Comrade Captain." The two clicked heels and left, closing the door behind them. Makeev locked it.

Beckoning with his pistol, Leonid Leonov indicated

the operating table, and said to Derek, "If you will please get up there, Colonel Inspector."

Derek hesitated, but there was nothing for it. There was no particular reason to get himself sapped upon everything else. He said, "What are you going to do?"

"You'll soon see," the captain said pleasantly. "Nothing that will hurt you—at this stage of the game. Nicholas, the sodium pentothal, I should think."

The second captain went over to one of the cases and returned with a vial and a hypodermic needle. He expertly knocked the tip off the glass vial and loaded the needle.

A hypodermic needle, Derek Lamb thought dully, how primitive could you get? He stretched out on the operating table. There were shackles on either side, but they didn't bother to utilize them. His chances of grabbing a weapon were disappearing by the moment. Both of them kept him carefully covered. Captain Makeev pressed the hypodermic into his right arm, then stepped back and threw it into a waste receptacle.

Captain Leonov said easily, "There'll be a slight wait, Colonel Inspector." He stepped back and took a chair, still imminently alert, his gun still at the ready. Makeev leaned against the wall and said, "What happened?"

His companion told him, in detail.

Makeev was surprised. "This should prove interesting."

Leonov looked at Derek. "What is your real name?" he said.

The Section G man's voice was empty. "Derek Lamb."

"What was your real planet of birth?"

"Mother Earth."

"Who do you really represent?"

"Section G, of the Bureau of Investigation, Department

of Justice, of the Commissariat of Interplanetary Affairs, of United Planets."

The two Stalinists looked at him for a long moment.

Finally, Leonov said, "What is your mission on Stalin?"

There was no possible way of his fighting it. Derek said, "To investigate the possibility of there being a need to overthrow the present government."

Both of the captains took deep breaths.

Leonov said, "I see. And, in view of Article One of the United Planets Charter, why is it deemed necessary on Mother Earth to investigate the possibility of overthrowing the Party's government here on Stalin?"

Derek Lamb said, his voice vastly empty, "Because it is possible that the present socioeconomic system is holding up scientific and technological progress."

Captain Makeev was scowling. He came over to the table upon which Derek was sprawled and looked down at him. "Why should the United Planets confederation care about progress on Stalin?"

"Because, unknown to the member planets, our Space Forces have discovered that there is other intelligent life in the galaxy. Sooner or later, we will confront them. They are far in advance of our own civilization. Mankind must make every effort to catch up to their level of technology, on the chance that they may not be . . . friendly."

The two Stalinists were obviously flabbergasted. They looked at each other.

Leonov said to his companion, "He can't be lying. He's under the sodium pentothal formula."

The other thought about it, and shook his head. He said to Derek, "And if you reported back to your Section G superiors that in your opinion there would be more progress on Stalin if the Party was overthrown, what would happen then?"

"I do not know."

Captain Makeev said impatiently, "What is most likely would happen?"

"They would most likely attempt to infiltrate a team of our agents to work toward the new revolution."

Leonov said, "And what would happen if you simply did not return."

"I do not know."

"What would most likely happen, damn it?"

"They would most likely make another attempt to send one of our agents in."

The two thought about that and then withdrew to the other side of the room and conferred in whispers. Finally, they returned and stared down at their victim.

Makeev said to Leonid Leonov, "Just what are our full instructions?"

"You heard them. We were to put him to the question, then shoot him and dispose of his body in the usual fashion, and then report in full to the Chairman."

Makeev said to Derek Lamb, "All right, come to your feet. Let's get going."

It was impossible for Derek to disobey. He wondered, in the near blankness of his mind, what had been in his injection besides the sodium pentothal. It was the most efficient truth serum, plus come-along, he had ever heard of.

He stood and awaited further orders.

Captain Leonov went to a door on the opposite side of the room from that through which they had entered, unlocked and then opened it.

"Through here," he said, his pistol still at the ready,

though he must have been fully aware of the fact that Derek was beyond a will of his own.

Derek preceded them, into a corridor similar to the other one they had come along. There were prison cells to each side.

He had read, in his studies or the early communists on Mother Earth of their system of execution in these political matters. They simply shot you in the back of the head, and disposed of your body secretly.

XV

The trip for Li Chang and Sid Jakes was an agony.

They were lobbed over to the Nuevo Albuquerque spaceport, and there they jittered while waiting for the small Space Forces craft which had to be recalled from Calisto.

"Isn't there any manner in which this could be speeded up?" Li Chang murmured, knowing as well as her colleague that there wasn't. They were seated at the bar of their hotel, nervously doing more drinking than was the wont of either of them.

Sid Jakes looked at her in understanding. "There is no speed in hyperspace, Li Chang, you know that. Before entering it, yes. After leaving it, yes. But in hyperspace itself there is no speed. The most sluggish freighter gets there as fast as the nattiest Space Forces one-man scout."

"Sam'll be on Doria two days before we arrive, then. Possibly three."

He didn't bother to answer that.

They spent most of their time on the *Gremlin* in the tiny mess. They tried to play some of the various games on board for the crew's relaxation, including battlechess, to kill the time, but couldn't concentrate. They sought out the ship's library and played tapes, but only the lightest

127

fictional things would come through. And even then they were hard put to follow the story line.

They must have been half way when Li Chang blurted, in the midst of a game that both had lost track of, "*Why?* Why is it that after all these centuries of supposed civilization we wind up with such worlds as Doria? Why should there be a need for a Section G, to attempt to contain such planets? How did they ever evolve? How can man be so stupid?"

"It's easy." Sid Jakes grinned sourly. "You know the answer as well as I do. Weren't you born in a commune, on the planet Han, settled by disgruntled followers of . . . what was his name, that early Chinese communist?"

"Mao," Li Chang murmured unhappily.

Sid Jakes grunted amusement. "The pioneers in space travel must never have dreamed of the method by which the suitable worlds would be colonized. Every group that figured they weren't getting a fair shake, took off like a bat out of hell for a world of their own." He chortled. "It was bad enough when outfits such as the anarchists settled their own planet, but you know what I ran into the other day?"

She looked at him. Anything to divert her mind.

He laughed ruefully. "A couple of thousand colonists with I.Q.s of less than one hundred. Some of them, considerably less. They figured they were a minority and had to take too much jetsam. So they founded their own society on their own world. They refuse to join United Planets, by the way."

Li Chang's face mirrored the nearest thing to a scowl of which it was capable. "But Sid," she said. "what in the world will happen to them?"

He shrugged. "Who knows? Perhaps they'll go back to

the Neanderthal. Or, who knows? Perhaps the ruggedness of existence will be such that they'll breed up their I.Q.s. Having a high I.Q. is no guarantee that your children will have one, or having a low one is no sign your children won't turn out geniuses. The fit will survive, the too stupid will go under. It's the way the race started."

She returned to her point. "But what I meant was, now humanity is faced with a common danger, the intelligent alien life form we've come in contact with. Why don't we meet it together, in all our strength?"

Sid chuckled ruefully, and gave up the game they hadn't been able to concentrate upon. He said, "Li Chang, Li Chang, you dreamer. Man stops being a thinking animal when you deal with his institutions, his subconscious beliefs, his religion. The Christians were willing to die in the arena before giving up their creed. The Aztecs fought it out, almost to the last man, although Cortez daily offered them surprisingly good terms, in view of the fact that they didn't have a chance. Hitler tried to the very last to bring down the whole Third Reich in flames, rather than surrender. Earlier in that same war, the Russian communists slugged it out, in such places as Stalingrad, long, long after the world thought that the Wehrmacht had defeated them.

"No, it's a fallacy to think man will give up his beliefs to meet a common danger. When the H-Bomb first threatened universal destruction, did man patch up his politico-economic difficulties? You know he didn't. *Better dead than red,* was one slogan, and the other side had just as strong ones. When the population explosion threatened to lead to complete chaos, did the old religions, the old institutions, in such lands as Europe and India change? Not by a long shot. They kept breeding like rabbits.

Man is at his most stubborn when his religious, socioeconomic, or political beliefs need change."

She sighed deeply and her eyes went back to the Tri-Di set, and she tried to find something that could hold their attention.

XVI

As Horsten, Helen and Lorans made their uncomfortable way across the open field, Lorans growled, "I suppose we should count our blessings. El Caudillo's government concentrates practically everything here in Nuevo Madrid. Suppose this confounded political prison was all the way on the other side of the planet."

Helen said, "I still don't know how we're going to locate them." She was perched up on Dorn Horsten's shoulder, as always when time had to be made.

Horsten said, "If we have this right, they keep their prime state prisoners in the left wing. Martha memorized it at the library."

Helen said, "Great, but there might be a thousand of them."

The doctor half stumbled over an unseen obstacle, caught his balance and said, "No. Contrary to the beliefs of most, police states don't necessarily have their prisons full. The worst political prisoners they shoot out of hand, the least dangerous they send off to slave labor projects. Why feed them in prison? Put them to work. Those in-between are kept in jail until it is decided if they belong to the first category, or second."

They had come to a wall. Pierre Lorans took a rope he

had been carrying and handed it to Helen. She wrapped one end of it around her waist turned to Dorn Horsten and said, "All right, you overgrown ox, Allez Oop."

He caught her, whirled, and released her in a surge of power, and she shot upward.

Even as the two men looked anxiously after the tiny mite, Lorans growled, "I wish I hadn't lost my boomerang, back there at the power station. What in the name of the Holy Ultimate will they think when they find it?"

"They won't think anything," Horsten grunted, still peering upward after his diminutive partner. "Until you showed me that damned thing, I'd never even heard of a boomerang, and I still don't quite believe the things you can do with it. There's no reason to believe that they've ever heard of them, either."

Lorans complained, "It was my favorite little tool. And one of the few we could take a chance on and bring along—in Helen's box of toys, of course. What's taking that girl so long?"

At that very moment, the end of the rope slithered down. Without further word, Doctor Horsten gave it a sharp tug or two, to make sure Helen had the other end well anchored, shoved his glasses firmly back on his nose, and then started up, hand over hand, his feet braced against the prison wall.

A few minutes later, the end of the rope jerked up and down in signal. Lorans took it and tied a loop in the end and put one foot inside. He gave a sharp double tug and was drawn upward to where the others awaited him on the wall top.

It was pitch dark.

Horsten whispered, "All right, let's go. We've seen a

132

few prison guards going about below with improvised lights. Evidently, the place is in a tizzy."

"Good," Lorans muttered. "The tizzier, the better."

Helen whispered, "Down this way, according to that chart Martha drew for us. The left wing is down this way."

They came to a barred door.

Horsten came to the front and inspected it. "The best thing," he murmured, even as his big hands went out, "is simply to break the . . ." he had grasped two of the heavy bars near the lock and suddenly pulled them toward him, ". . . lock." With a rip of tortured metal, the door came open toward him.

Lorans winced. "How about alarms?"

"Don't be silly," Helen told him. "What do you think we fouled up that power plant for? Now let me go on ahead and scout this out."

The two men pressed back against the wall while she reconnoitered. She took longer to return than they found reasonable, so when she did show, both felt considerable relief. She was breathing deeply.

"What happened?" Lorans demanded.

"I ran into two guards and had to clobber them."

The doctor looked down at her tiny figure and shook his head. "I'll never get used to it," he muttered under his breath.

Helen said, "I found out where they are."

"Where who are?"

"Don't be dense. Our boys. Hoyos and Guerro."

The two men stared at her. "How'd you find that out?" Lorans said.

"Oh, one of the two guards," Helen said lightly. "Down this way."

"Just a minute," Doctor Horsten said coldly. "What did you go to the guard? I like to know what's behind me before I go into something."

She tried to brush it off. "I just kind of twisted his arm a little."

For a brief moment, Doctor Dorn Horsten had before his eyes the picture of this seemingly sweet little girl putting strong arm methods to work on a tough, burly prison guard until the other divulged information.

He said, "You mean you let him see you, clearly?"

Helen shrugged it off. "So what? You think he's going to report to his chief that an eight-year-old girl put the slug on him?"

They gave up and followed her. From time to time, through windows overlooking the prison yard below, they could see guards, or other prison employees, going this way and that with lanterns, flashlights or torches. Civilized institutions fall apart drastically without power.

Helen whispered, "This way . . . I think."

Back at the hotel, they returned to the Lorans suite by much the same manner as they had scaled the prison wall. But this time there were an extra two members of the party.

After Horsten had made it up the wall, he hauled the others after him, one, two, three. Helen, of course, had gone first, propelled by her hefty partner.

Martha was there, ready with a drink all around, a good stiff slug of Falange cognac.

Pierre Lorans said to her, "Anything while we were gone, my dear?"

She said, "No. Not so much as a knock on the door."

Lorans turned to the two newcomers. "If you'll come

this way, we'll get you out of that prison garb and get some new clothes on you. Later, either the doctor or I will take those you're wearing out and dispose of them." He led the continually surprised Falangist underground men to his bedroom.

Meanwhile, Dorn Horsten opened the door to the hall and bellowed out into the darkness, "Hallow! Damn it, how long is this fantastic situation going to last! We want lights, food, something to drink! Hallow! Damn it!"

Eventually, a hotel servant, bearing a heavy candle, came scurrying and the scientist made a big to-do about sitting around in the dark for the past couple of hours, and that they demanded some service.

The servant scurried off again. He gave the impression of having been doing a lot of scurrying all evening.

The doctor gave a grunt of satisfaction and turned back to Martha and Helen. "It'll never occur to anybody that we haven't been here all evening," he said.

"We hope," Helen muttered.

Lorans returned with the two liberated prisoners and the next fifteen minutes was expended explaining to the revolutionaries the purpose of the Lorans-Horsten team and the scheme to keep the two safely hidden by their remaining out in the open, disguised as waiters.

The older of the two, Bartolome Guerro, was a tall, all but gaunt, Andulusian type, dark of complexion, inclined to flare in his speech. He was obviously a leader of men. The other, to the surprise of the Section G operatives, was a youngster, certainly not beyond his early twenties. Of medium height, he moved with a litheness seldom found in men and he seemed incapable of making an awkward movement.

It came out in the conversation. Jose Hoyos, full matador at the age of eighteen, had been the last, despairing hope of the Lorca Party, an illegal underground organization dedicated to the overthrow of the entire El Caudillo system. Even before the coming of the Section G operative who had worked with them, they had sought out this potential champion from the ranks of the organization. Jose was a third generation son of a family devoted to the building of a new world-government to supersede the present system on Falange. His reflexes were fast, his appearance strikingly handsome, his grace, superlative. Helen could hardly keep her eyes off him.

The Falangist underground had groomed him for the next series of national games, when the old Caudillo had died and a new one was to be selected. The idea was to have him acclaimed El Caudillo and then to make sweeping changes from within. They had gathered funds to see him through the best of the planet's bullfighting schools. They had gone to the expense of advancing his career through the *novillero* years, when, as an amateur, it was so difficult for the usual torero to find fights, it often being necessary that the young hopeful buy his own bull to be fought.

They had backed his career for years, waiting, waiting, and step by step Jose Hoyos had reached prominence, until in the opinion of most *aficionados* he was Numbero Tres, third man from the top in the lists of matadors. The two above him were gentlemen toreros, both at least ten years his senior and both the epitome of the hero of the fiesta brava, national spectacle of the planet Falange.

They had arrived then, at a position of having only to wait for the demise of the present Caudillo for Jose to have his chance. Needless to say, El Caudillo, though no longer a young man, was in no hurry.

136

The lean Bartolome Guerro looked around at the Section G operatives. "It was then your colleague, Phil Birdman, came to Falange and stressed the importance of dispatch. He couldn't wait for the Caudillo's natural death."

Martha said, "You mean he favored assassination?" There was discomfort in her voice. "Only in very extreme cases does Section G ever condone that."

The Falangist looked at her. "Not necessarily. It would be impossible to assassinate El Caudillo. His security is simply too embracing. Birdman was trying to find some other method of speeding things. Perhaps there would be some manner of inducing him to retire."

Horsten shook his head. They were talking now by the light of a small fire Pierre Lorans had built in the fireplace. He said, "Any public figure can be assassinated, given a determined enough group, with adequate resources."

The youthful Hoyos, usually silent, spoke up. "Not El Caudillo," he said. "His police are as thick as soup."

The doctor grunted. "Of course, I don't advocate political assassinations," he said, "but listen to this one. Some centuries ago on Earth, a desperate radical political group decided it was necessary to kill a titled foreigner who was to have a parade in their city. Troops and police, they knew, would be present in literally tens of thousands. So twenty-five of their number gathered in a room and drew straws and the five who had the shortest were given bombs or pistols and were told where to spot themselves along the path of the parade. Then they left. Those twenty remaining drew straws. The five with the shortest were given pistols and instructed to place themselves behind the appointed assassins, in the crowd. If, when it came the

137

turn of one of the assassins to make his try at the victim, he failed to try, then the man stationed behind him was to shoot him. Those five then left and the remaining men drew straws and the five with the shortest were given pistols and instructed to stand behind the second man. If the first man failed to make his try, and the second man refrained from shooting the first, then it was the task of the third to shoot the second. These five left and straws were chosen again. The five short ones were issued pistols , and instructed to stand behind the third man in the crowd, and if the first man failed to make his try and the second man failed to shoot him, and the third man failed to shoot the second, then the fourth man's task was to shoot the third man. The five remaining men, need not, of course, draw straws. They issued themselves guns and left to assume their posts—behind the fourth man."

The doctor let his eyes go around the group. "The next day, the parade started on schedule. The automobile containing the titled visitor and his wife reached the first assassin who attempted to throw his bomb but was caught by the police. It reached the second assassin who tried to shoot them with his pistol, but was pulled down by the surrounding mob. They reached the third assassin— and got no further."

Horsten held his peace for a moment, and then said, "The assassins claimed their victim but they didn't know what the cost was to be. His name was Archduke Ferdinand Hapsburg, and his death precipitated the first of the World Wars."

Bartolome Guerro thought about it. Finally, he said, "Why did you tell us of this?"

The big scientist shrugged. "Merely pointing out that

138

dedicated men can do what must be done. Your problem here, of course, is different."

"Yes, of course." The Falangist revolutionist stirred in his chair. "Jose and I must get out and reestablish our contacts, get in touch with the cells of our Nuevo Madrid organization. Our arrest caused considerable disruption of long laid-plans."

Horsten said, "One thing. Our central offices have decided that the government of El Caudillo stands in the way of progress, but there is no point in tearing down one socioeconomic system unless a superior one is available to take its place. What is your own philosophy of government, Senor Guerro?"

The gaunt man took his time. Finally, he said "Government should be by the elite, nothing else makes sense. Who wishes to be led by someone competent only to bring up the rear? But each generation must find its own elite. They are not necessarily and automatically the children of the last generation's, nor are they necessarily to be found among those with titles, great traditions behind them, nor accumulated wealth."

Both Horsten and the Lorans were nodding their basic agreement. The doctor said, "And what is your method of selecting your governing elite?"

The Falangist looked full into his eyes and said very slowly, "This is an internal problem of our world. We will solve it based on local conditions, needs, traditions —all the factors that make Falange unique." His voice went slower still. "We do not need the assistance of even friends from worlds beyond, where our institutions and temperaments are not fully understood. We thank you for your cooperation in destroying the corrupt govern-

139

ment of El Caudillo, but we must insist on being the engineers of our own future."

"Damn well put," Helen said.

"And now we must go," Guerro said.

Martha said worriedly, "You'll be safe? We planned to keep you here for the time."

Guerro and Hoyos came to their feet. "We'll be as safe as can be expected," Guerro said. "Your group will continue to remain here?"

"Yes," Dorn Horsten said, "Our cover is excellent. When your people have come to some plan of action, let us know. Meanwhile, we shall put our own minds to the situation."

Jose Hoyos was looking down at Helen speculatively.

There was an element of apology in his voice when he asked, "How old are you truly?"

Helen was snappish. "That is a question no man should ever ask a woman."

He looked down at her again, taking in the little girl's dress, sprinkled with wild flowers, at the blonde hair caught up in its ribbon. He shook his head.

"You want to Indian wrestle?" she snarled.

"I beg your pardon?" The good looking torero was confused.

"Leave him alone, Helen," Martha sighed.

"I'll clobber him," Helen muttered under her breath, in a voice that was neither childish nor ladylike. "How long am I supposed to go between dates in this damned Section G! I'm a normal young woman."

They saw the two Falangist citizens to the door, the Doctor checking the hall up and down, before letting them go. He said, "In this dark, you'll get through the lobby without trouble."

When they were gone, Helen leaned her back against the door and said, "Holy Jumping Zen, but he's beautiful. You should have seen his eyes pop when I wiggled through the bars of his cell."

Colonel Segura did what little there was in his power to make his voice sound soothing. He was seated in the gray drabness of his office, his heavy Castilian desk a litter of papers and reports, a heavy military revolver used as a paperweight to hold down a pile to his right.

He said now, "No loyal *ciudadano* need fear the officials of El Caudillo's government. They need only tell the truth and receive the acclaim of El Caudillo's faithful servants."

The man before him squirmed. In his time, the other had run afoul of El Caudillo's faithful servants before. Never seriously, though any contact at all with the *Policia Secreta* was serious enough. But he had never dreamed —save possibly in nightmare—that he would ever confront Miguel Segura himself. One heard stories of Miguel Segura. They were far from being reassuring stories.

"Now," the colonel said in heavy gentleness, "just what was it you saw?"

"Senor Colonel, I was taking a walk through the park. . . ."

The colonel nodded, and his voice was not quite so gentle. "So I understand. At perhaps two o'clock in the morning."

The other squirmed again. "Senor Colonel, I can explain. My wife and I. . . ."

Segura held up an impatient hand. "I am not at present interested in why a supposedly honest *ciudadano* might

141

find fit to prowl the streets in the dead of night. Get to your story."

"Senor Colonel, it is unbelievable."

The colonel was beginning to lose patience. He said, "There have been many unbelievable things happening in this city recently. Quick now!"

"Senor Colonel, your Excellency. I was not drunk."

"Your story!" the colonel roared.

The other faltered, took a deep breath. "Senor Colonel, I saw a man walk up the side of the Posada San Francisco."

"You saw *what*?"

"Senor Colonel, I was not drunk. I insist. When I told my wife, she told a neighbor. Soon it had spread throughout the block and the *Guardia Civil* came to question me, as they always come to question if there is the slightest deviation from every day routine."

"All right. What do you mean, you saw a man walk up the side of the Posada San Francisco? You mean he was climbing up the side of the hotel, do you not?"

The man was in a sweat. He said, or rather stuttered, "Senor Colonel, it was at a distance, one admits. It was none too clear. But it was a man and he was not climbing. Not in the ordinary sense. He was *walking* up the wall. He got to the fourth, or perhaps the fifth, floor and then disappeared."

"Disappeared?" the colonel rasped. "You mean that he went into a window?"

"Perhaps. For me, he simply disappeared."

The colonel stared at the other for a long unprofitable minute. The other was no more capable of lying to him than he was of flying. He said finally, "Could it have been that he had a rope suspended from the window and was climbing it, walking up the wall holding onto such a rope?"

"Perhaps, Senor Colonel. It was at a distance, as I have already said."

Get out," the colonel said. "Leave your complete story with the sergeant outside."

After his informant had left, the colonel sat for a long time, staring unseeingly into a far corner of the office, his face working. A light flashed on his desk. He pressed a button.

Teniente Raul Dobarganes entered, a curved piece of wood in hand. The thing might have been a meter in length in all, it might possibly have been a club, but if so, it was an unlikely looking one.

Sugera growled a sour welcome, then, "Well, Raul what in the name of the Holy Ultimate is it?"

"It is a boomerang."

The colonel looked at him.

Raul Dobarganes cleared his throat. "A weapon of the Australian Aborigines."

"You are telling me nothing. What is an Australian whatever-you-said?"

"A very primitive people of Mother Earth. Evidently, according to my historical informant, the device also showed up on other parts of ancient Mother Earth. They were even found in Egyptian tombs. One form of the boomerang was more a toy than anything else. You threw it and it made a large circle out into the air and then returned to you."

The colonel looked at the instrument again as though unbelieving but kept his peace.

His lieutenant went on. "The hunting and war boomerangs were different. They were meant to strike the

143

game, or enemy, at a distance and with great accuracy and force."

"You mean you simply threw the thing? Why should it be any more accurate than any other, well, club?"

"It twirls in the air." The young aide demonstrated, twisting the stick. "Going around and around like this. The way it is twisted, the wood, it evidently acts as some sort of air foil."

"Let me see that damned thing," the colonel snapped, taking it.

He handled it, stared down at it.

Finally he snapped. "Get me the customs report on the possessions brought in by Pierre Lorans and his family and by Doctor Horsten. Check back to make double sure that the inspection was as thorough as usual. I want to know if as much as a single toothpick could have gotten past undetected."

"Yes, Colonel Segura," his aide said, about faced and hurried for the door.

When the reports came, the colonel poured over them with a feeling of frustration. He didn't know what he was looking for. Nevertheless, he found it eventually.

He stabbed with his finger, accusingly. "A box of toys."

Raul Dobarganes didn't know what to make of that.

"What toys?" the colonel rasped.

"Why . . . why, a girl's toys, I suppose," his aide said. "Toys for that little girl, dolls and so forth."

"Ha!" the colonel said. "Put a man in the Lorans suite at the first opportunity. When they are at dinner, or something. I want to know what's in that box of supposed toys. Also check thoroughly on that confounded microphone that is continually breaking. And another thing, Raul. That electrician from the Posada. Have him

144

in here. And that guard from the archives who had the fanciful story of half a dozen men descending upon him from the skies. Bring him here. And those hysterical guards from the Alcazar Prison. I want them too. On the double, Raul!"

His assistant was interrupted for one last order. "And, Raul. You might get in touch with that Temple Monk assigned to the task of exorcising the poltergeists at the city power plant. You can tell him it won't be necessary."

"Yes, Colonel Segura," Raul Dobarganes said, bewildered.

Colonel Segura bent a baleful eye on the night guard of the archives of the *Policia Secreta*. He said, and there was an infinite cold in his voice, "This time I want the true story of what happened that night the safe was stolen."

"Senor Colonel. . . ." There were blisters of cold sweat on the man's forehead. If anything, he seemed more distraught than he had been the night of the crime. Evidently, he'd had time to think it over in detail and the thinking hadn't reassured him. Which was interesting, the colonel decided.

The colonel said, "Your life is at stake. I want the truth."

"Senor Colonel, I told the truth. Most of it is a mystery to me. They descended upon me from I know not where. Seemingly from the air. I was helpless, immediately."

"How many of them did you say there were?"

The guard's eyes darted, but there was no escape. "I . . . I don't know, Senor Colonel."

The colonel leaned forward ominously. "Were there, perhaps, only two . . . or three?"

145

SECTION G: UNITED PLANETS

The blisters of sweat had evolved into rivulets of sweat so that the man had to wipe them away desperately.

The colonel's eyes shot suddenly to his lieutenant. "Put him to the torture," he rasped.

"No . . . no . . ." the guard squealed.

"Torture him. I want every tiny detail of what really happened in that archives room."

"Yes, Colonel," Raul Dobarganes said unhappily. He didn't like this phase of his work. He put his head out the office door and summoned four plainclothesmen.

"No . . . no . . ." the victim was still squealing his protests as they hauled him off.

The colonel's mouth was working again. "Now those prison wardens who allowed the subversives to escape. Bring them in. I want a rehash of that story too."

Martha Lorans looked out the window and said, "Oh, oh."

"What's the matter?" Helen said.

"Come here, quick. That line of men, crossing the park."

Helen took one look and said quickly, "Get Pete," and darted for the door, the hall, and the suite of Dorn Horsten.

She made it only half way. Suddenly, from around the corner of the hotel corridor, two brawny *Policia Secreta* men, both carrying pistols, grabbed her.

Kicking and squealing, she was carried off unceremoniously.

Back in the Lorans apartment, Pierre entered from an inner room. "What's the matter?"

Martha said hurriedly, "Pierre, armed men are closing

146

in from all sides. It must be for us. Is there any last thing we can do? Are there any papers to burn or——"

"No, of course not. All of our papers are in your head. Where's Helen and Dorn . . . ?"

"She's gone to get him. Do you think there's any way we can get out of here?"

"No," he said in disgust. "But we can try. Come on, Martha!"

He headed for the door, she immediately behind him.

It opened and they were confronted by Colonel Segura. Behind him were at least a dozen armed men.

"Ah," the colonel said politely. "The Cordon Bleu chef who doesn't appreciate the cuisine of Falange, eh? We shall see what you think of the food we serve the inmates of Alcazar Prison, especially those sentenced to be shot for illegal activities against the government of El Caudillo."

There were sounds of a battle royal going on down the hall; great shouts, breaking of furniture, cries of agony.

The colonel turned to one of his minions. "Take four more men with stun-guns. A freak who can carry a 600 pound safe down ten flights of stairs and then tear the door off, evidently with his bare hands, can take a lot of subduing. Be sure not to kill him. We have a great deal to find out about this operation."

He turned back to the Lorans. "You will accompany me to the *Policia Secreta* headquarters for interrogation."

Pierre Lorans said, "This is an outrage. I wish to inform the United Planets Embassy of my arrest, so that I can arrange for an attorney for our defense."

Some police underling in the background chuckled at that.

147

SECTION G: UNITED PLANETS

The colonel said formally, "Pierre Lorans, you are unfamiliar with Falange legal procedure. The court will appoint an attorney to handle your defense."

"A Falange attorney?" Lorans snorted, drawing himself up in his Gallic stance. "I want a United Planets lawyer."

Martha said lowly, "That's their law, Pierre. The court appoints defense lawyers in cases involving subversion and espionage."

They were marched into the hall where they were met by another delegation of Policia Secreta, these carrying a trussed up Helen. Still further along the hall came two *Guardia Civil,* looking the worse for wear. They carried a stretcher and upon it, unconscious and breathing deeply, Doctor Dorn Horsten.

A service elevator took them down to street level, and they emerged in service quarters and then into an alley behind the hotel. Police limousines awaited them there and they were whisked to the large, dark, dominating *Policia Secreta* building which Helen and Horsten had penetrated so short a time ago, looking for the court records of the trial of the Section G agent.

They were hurried through passages, into a large gloomy interrogation room.

Pierre, Martha and Helen were pushed into chairs. The colonel eyed the now stirring Doctor Horsten. He said to his bully-boys, "Two of you station yourselves across the room with your guns trained on him. If he shows any belligerence at all, stun him again."

The doctor, groaning from the aftermaths of the blasts he had received earlier, revived rather quickly, once the process had started. His bones felt as though he had suffered rheumatism and arthritis for a decade and more. He rubbed them painfully, even as he looked up.

He managed to get out, in indignation, "What is the meaning of this? Do you have a warrant for this outrage?"

"A technicality we dispense with on Falange, my good Doctor, and as temporary residents you come under our legal code. All of our laws apply to you," the colonel told him smoothly. And now, just so as not to waste time, let me inform you that your trial will take place within the hour, and you will be shot this afternoon, at latest. Between then and now, you will be placed on Scop, truth serum, to reveal any accomplices you may have had in your vicious schemes."

"Some trial that's going to be, if you already know we're going to be shot," Helen said bitterly. She made no effort to maintain her childish treble.

The colonel looked at her and made a mocking bow. "I have not forgotten the kick you gave me, Senorita Lorans." He afforded a light laugh. "Our investigation tells us that there is a whole planet of people such as yourself, though evidently you are one of the top gymnasts. A champion acrobat on a world that loves gymnastics. It explains a great deal of what would have seemed unexplainable." He turned to the doctor. "And you, Dorn Horsten. We have a bit of information on your own home planet, ah, Brobdingnag. It must be a strange world, indeed."

The doctor said, "I'd like to get just two fingers around your neck."

"I am sure you would," the colonel smiled in most friendly fashion. "But time presses. The court is being set up for your ever so brief trial. So immediately we will resort to our Scop——"

Teniente Raul Dobarganes burst open the door to interrupt him. He came in, his face ghost-pale.

149

SECTION G: UNITED PLANETS

"What in the name of the Holy Ultimate is wrong?" his superior snapped at him.

Raul Dobarganes shook his head, as though to achieve clarity. "El Caudillo," he whispered. "El Caudillo has been shot. He is dead."

XVII

Derek Lamb and his captors came to one cell which seemed somewhat larger and not quite so grim as the others. Besides the toilet facilities, it had a small table, two chairs, and a steel bunk with an army blanket.

Captain Leonov motioned to the bunk. "Stretch out there and go to sleep."

Even in his inability to think clearly Derek Lamb was surprised. What were they waiting for? Why didn't they shoot him immediately—in the back of the head, as tradition demanded? He stretched out, as ordered, and dimly realized that they were leaving, locking the cell door behind them. Escape, when the drug had worn off? No. Even if he escaped the cell, how was he to get out of these prison cellars? And, if he did, how was he to get out of the palace of the Chairman of the Presidium? And, if he did, how was he to get out of this fortress? And, if he did, how was he to get off the planet Stalin? He fell asleep. There is one advantage to knowing that death is certain; you don't have to worry about it any more.

When he awoke, the two captains were seated at the table, watching him. Their guns were holstered. Their legs were crossed and there was the inevitable—on the planet Stalin—bottle of vodka on the table. It was about half empty. They had obviously been sitting there for a time.

Derek Lamb shook his head in an attempt to clear it. The effects of the truth serum had worn off. He couldn't think of anything to say. However, it was their ball, and he assumed that they'd start bouncing it.

Captain Leonid Leonov said without tone in his voice, "You're awake. Do you feel all right?"

It was roughly the last question that Derek had expected to hear. Why in hell should the damned Stalinist care how he felt? He said, "I suppose so. When does the execution take place?"

They ignored that. Nicholas Makeev said, "Do you think it will work?"

Derek Lamb was capable of exasperation. He said, "Do I think what will work?"

The Stalinist captain said, "This plan of United Planets to accelerate progress on all the human-settled worlds, in anticipation of eventual confrontation with the intelligent aliens you told us about."

Derek swung his legs around and to the floor and sat up on the edge of the bunk. He ran a shaky forefinger over his slightly protrudent front teeth and stared at the others.

Leonov repeated his companion's words. "Do you think that it will work?"

"How in the hell would I know?" Derek said wearily. "Possibly it's dependent upon how much time we have to develop our science. Our race is expanding to new worlds every Earth year that goes by. Some of these colonists will, sooner or later, run into the aliens. Then the fat will be in the fire, if they're hostile, which they most

152

likely will be. But what else can we do? We can't just sit back and wait. We've got to do everything we can to prepare."

"Of course," Captain Leonid Leonov said, nodding.

Derek bug-eyed him.

Makeev said, very thoughtfully, "It will mean that it will be necessary to speed things up here on Stalin."

Derek turned his stare to him. "Speed what thing up?" he demanded.

"The counterrevolution," Leonov said reasonably.

Derek Lamb closed his eyes in pain, and in mute appeal to higher powers.

He opened them again and said, "What counterrevolution?"

Makeev said, "Derek Lamb, you have been on Stalin but a few hours, however, you have surely noted how inefficiently the planet is run, how inadequate our leaders are. From time to time there have been efforts to overthrow them, and always in the past such efforts have ended in a bloodbath. This time, we were using new tactics, but we weren't quite ready to act. Now, your advent and your information on the crisis confronting our species makes it necessary to . . . speed things up."

Derek Lamb said, "Look, could I have a slug of that vodka?" He came to his feet and approached the table.

Leonov laughed and poured a drink into one of the three tumblers. Derek shakily knocked it back, then returned to his seat on the bunk.

He said, "All right. What new tactics? Perhaps I can help. I've spent quite a few years of my life working at revolution and revolt on various worlds. And behind me, I have an organization that specializes in such matters."

153

SECTION G: UNITED PLANETS

They looked at him questioningly. "Perhaps you can at that," Captain Leonov said softly.

The Stalinist thought about it for a moment, then said, "I'll start at the beginning, Derek Lamb. When N. Lenin overthrew the Czarist regime in Russia, the men he led, the Old Bolsheviks, were both dedicated and capable. After Lenin's death, Stalin, with his bureaucracy, took over and what remained of Lenin's old comrades were finished off."

He hesitated before going on. "There's something that happens in a self-perpetuating bureaucracy. The first generation is possibly quite efficient, but what they do is practice favoritism and nepotism. The sons and daughters of the ruling elite are sent to the best schools and groomed to take over the positions of the bureaucracy. It might work reasonably well, in the second generation, but by the time the third, fourth, fifth generation comes along, it is not necessarily the most competent persons who are running your bureaucratic state. In fact, it's very unlikely. Rather than the best men getting the top, it's your party leaders. So it was in the Soviet Union. By the time the country had become industrialized and computerized, the need was for efficient scientists and technicians to be in power, but instead, the old bureaucracy was still in the saddle."

Derek said impatiently, "All this isn't exactly news to me, Captain."

"I was but giving you background. In Russia, the bureaucracy was finally eliminated, but when my ancestors came here to the planet Stalin, they brought the old institutions with them. Ever since there have been some elements in our population that have tried to overthrow the bureaucracy and get this world back on the path to progress."

"But what are these new tactics you spoke of?"

Makeev said, "We're infiltrating them, this time. And, at the same time, we are doing all we can to encourage their worst elements."

Derek eyed him, not understanding. "Encourage. . . ."

"Yes," the other nodded. "You see, when the crisis comes, it is better for us to have such stupid people as Alex Vavilov as chairman of the presidium, than someone more efficient. Another thing is that in order to function at all, Vavilov has to surround himself with such people as myself and Leonid, here. And the only source of such people is our counterrevolutionary organization."

The Section G agent said slowly, "So, in actuality, you are already running the country. The Party is a facade."

Leonov nodded acceptance of that. "What you say is largely correct."

"Then why don't you simply take over?"

The Stalinist nodded again. "As I said, there have been attempts in the past that always ended in bloodbaths. This time we want to be absolutely sure. Can your Section G help?"

Derek Lamb considered. He said, finally, "Could your people infiltrate the artificial satellite, take it over completely, so only your own people were aboard?"

Makeev and Leonov thought it over. Leonov said finally, a bit hesitantly, "I would think so. Already, practically all the technicians are members of our organization. Actually, we'd only have to get rid of Major Kulski. We could replace him with one of our own."

"If you could do that, Section G could send you any

155

equipment you might need—weapons, manpower of the type fully acquainted with putting over a revolt. But the trouble is, I have no way of communicating with Earth. I was afraid to bring a Section G communicator since it might have been found."

"That's no problem. You're going back."

"How?" Derek said disgustedly. "It will probably be months before another freighter touches that satellite of yours, and even when one does come, how would I get up to it, and past the guards and so on?"

Makeev grinned at him, the first time Derek Lamb had seen any humor in the man. "We have been in contact with Captain Simack, of the *Goddard*. He is now orbiting the planet. We have a hidden space shuttle, less than a hundred kilometers from Stalingrad. It is meant for emergency escape, if any of us are discovered. Very well, we'll send you up to the *Goddard*. In fact, we had better get going right away. We can't expect Captain Simack to await you indefinitely." The two captains stood.

Leonov poured them each a last stiff drink, and they took up their glasses.

Something came to Derek and he said, "Look, what did you tell Chairman Vavilov?"

Makeev grinned again. "Oh, we did up a very complete report for him. You were an interplanetary fugitive from justice, wanted for everything from murder to rape. The United Planets police were after you, so you faked papers hoping you could go to ground here on Stalin for a prolonged period."

"Holy Jumping Zen," Derek said. "What did he say?"

"He wanted to know how you had taken being shot."

Derek looked at him.

"You took it like a man."

Derek held up his glass in toast. "That's good," he said. "Well, Long Live the Revolution."

Leonov amended him only slightly. "Long Live the *New* Revolution," he said.

XVIII

Li Chang and Sid Jakes were met at the Doria space-port by what could have been described as an honor guard of twenty men. However, they had no illusions. Before landing, the ensign who skippered the four man crew of the little *Gremlin* had been required to state the purpose of the set down, and to enumerate the passengers who expected to disembark. They had made no effort to disguise their identities, if for no other reason than that there had been no time to improvise a cover, had that been possible, considering the craft in which they had arrived.

The guard snapped to attention, and presented arms, as Li Chang Chu and Sid Jakes emerged from the United Planets Space Forces ship.

A nattily uniformed officer approached and came to the salute. "Supervisor Jakes, Supervisor Chu," he clipped out. "Welcome to Doria."

Sid Jakes grinned at him, ruefully. "Hi, Desmond." He held out a hand.

The other hesitated, then shook. "It's been a long time, Sid."

Sid Jakes turned to Li Chang and said, "Do you two know each other?"

Desmond bowed over her hand. "We operated in different sections, but I have heard a great deal about Supervisor Chu."

Li Chang said demurely, "Thank you."

Sid Jakes chuckled. "We hardly expected quite this reception, Desmond. How are the rest of the boys?"

The other was a man in his mid-thirties. Healthy; at least on the surface, adjusted and at ease. His eyes were as clear as those of his former superior. He smiled, a faint mocking quality in the background. "Like myself. For the first time in life, really happy and at peace with themselves. Doria is a great planet, Sid."

The smile on Sid Jakes's face faded. He said, his voice slightly tight, "Nothing like being coked to the gills to make the world rosy."

But the Dorian security officer only laughed. "If you don't understand it, Sid, don't knock it. Somebody once wrote that censors were mostly illiterates. Suffice to say, we former Section G agents, now serving El Primero, are considerably happier than when we were taking orders from Ross Metaxa and trying to live up to the way *he* thought things ought to be."

Sid said snappishly, "And does El Primero needle himself with the same happy dust he gives you?"

There was the most distant of glints in the other's eye, but he said, still pleasantly, "Sid, you remind me of those fat old ladies I saw on a historical fiction Tri-Di show not so long ago. They belonged to an outfit called the WCTU, an anti-alcohol organization. They'd beat the drums against drinking guzzle and then after the meeting serve refreshments of cakes, cookies, pies, candy and well-sweetened lemonade or tea. I imagine nobody ever got around to telling them that alcohol and sugar do much

159

the same thing in the human body. After the meeting, they'd go home and lie around, eating chocolates and fouling up their health by going to lard."

Li Chang said mildly, "There are some small differences between guzzle and candy."

Desmond looked at her. He said, "Either, taken moderately, won't hurt you. Either taken in excess, can jetsam your health, irreparably." He switched the subject. "May I ask that you accompany me to Interrogation? A formality, upon landing on Doria."

They followed. A non-commissioned officer bit out a command and the guard very briskly wheeled and fell in behind.

On the edge of the field, they entered an attractive administration building and, now followed only by the non-com and two of his men, proceeded down a short hall to a door lettered, in small, simple gold type, *Interrogation*.

The room beyond was most comfortably furnished. A desk, several comfortable chairs, a small bar in a corner.

The ex-Section G agent went through the formalities, held a chair for Li Chang, offered them both a drink, which they refused in view of the morning hour. He finally took his place behind the desk. The two soldiers had remained outside the door. The non-com had entered behind them and stood to one side, his face expressionless; however, his side arm was in a quick-draw holster.

Sid Jakes said testily, "You had the last word on that WCTU thing, and that, 'if you don't comprehend it, don't knock it,' routine. Would you mind elaborating?"

"Not at all," Desmond smiled. "You've got the United Planets dream, Jakes. I've got the Dorian dream. It's an easier dream. All we want is for Doria to be left alone, and leave others alone, including any bogeyman alien life forms. You're patriotic—the old term. You come from Earth, the mother planet. You bleed for Earth and want to impose on all the rest of humanity-settled planets, the things that Earth stands for. To accomplish this, you beat the drums about the need to unite against an alien foe. It's a new takeoff on the old Roman adage, if you have trouble at home, stir up war abroad."

"You think patriotism is stupid?"

Desmond smiled still once again. "It's according to what epoch you're living in. In early society, it was a necessity if the tribe—or, later, the city-state—was to survive. But in later societies, when indulged in, it meant suicide for the whole race."

Li Chang said hesitantly, "I don't believe that I quite follow that."

The Dorian security officer looked at her and nodded. "In the old days, before man had left his home world, you had a multitude of nations. A man would say, "I'm proud to be an Englishman. God Save the King. I'm patriotic. I'd die for England." And often he did. Why was he proud to be an Englishman? He hadn't done anything to achieve that status. By an accident of fate, he had parents who were living in England at the time of his birth. Had he been born in India, he could then have been proud of being an Indian, and willing to kill other nationalities—including English—in the name of patriotism. It particularly became nonsense, after the advent of nuclear fission."

He waved a hand negatively. "Patriotism belongs to the childhood of the race. But let us get to the point. The purpose of your landing on Doria. In view of your office. . . ."

Sid Jakes said, "I'll be glad to tell you all about it."

161

Desmond nodded. "Do you mind if I put a truth beam on you?"

Sid Jakes hesitated only momentarily. "Of course not."

A light, centered on the desk, lit up, white.

Desmond said, "In the way of test: Are you opposed to the government of El Primero?"

"Yes," Sid said.

The light burned green.

The security officer smiled lightly and said, "Do you think Supervisor Li Chang Chu an ugly woman?"

Sid grinned. "Yes," he said. "Very ugly."

The light burned red and both Desmond and Li Chang smiled.

Desmond smilingly said, "Have you stopped beating your mother?"

Sid chuckled. "Well, yes and no."

The light remained white.

Desmond said, his voice sharper now, "What is the purpose of your visit to Doria?"

"To apprehend a killer and return with him to Earth, before he can commit a murder."

The Dorian security officer's eyes widened infinitesimally, and he darted a glance at the light which turned green.

He said, "Where did the killer come from?"

"Earth." The light was green.

"You say he came here to kill someone?"

"Yes." The light was green.

"Who?"

Sid Jakes said, very slowly, "El Primero, Michael Ortega." The light was green.

The other was suddenly on his feet, his face chalk, his voice shrill. "That is impossible!"

162

SECTION G: UNITED PLANETS

Sid Jakes shook his head. "Do you think that I, assistant to Commissioner Metaxa, would be here on a mission less important?"

The other, his eyes bugging, leaned over the desk, his fists supporting him. "Section G has been trying to destroy El Primero and his government. Do you contend that now you are trying to prevent him from being assassinated?"

Sid Jakes said evenly, "Supervisor Chu and I have come from Earth to save the life of the present El Primero."

The light burned green.

The other stared at it, momentarily, then brought his eyes back to the Section G second-in-command. "It is impossible to assassinate El Primero. His security is impregnable. Even now he is preparing to address the entire population on a matter of the utmost importance, but he will never leave the palace grounds."

Li Chang spoke softly. "Do you think we are not familiar with all this, Citizen? But no security can thwart this killer. That is why we are here."

The light burned green, acknowledging the truth of her statement.

The other slumped back in his chair, his mouth working, a trickle of saliva at its side.

"Sir!" the non-com said anxiously.

"Shut up!" his superior rasped. Then to Jakes, "Who? Who is this killer?"

Sid Jakes shook his head. "I must have assurance that if and when we apprehend him, we will be allowed to return with him to Earth."

"No! No, we of the Dorian police will see to him. We protect El Primero with our lives. Our very souls!"

Sid Jakes shook his head again. "This is not an ordinary assassin, Desmond. You have not the time to put pressure on us. He may strike momentarily. Your guarantee, sent in a subspace cable to the Octagon, on Earth, that he will be put in our custody, or we do not reveal his identity. Otherwise, I guarantee the present El Primero will die shortly."

The light burned green, and the security officer once again stared unbelievingly at it.

Psycho-altered he might be, but his reflexes were still the same as those required years before, when his application as a Section G operative had been accepted. He flicked on an orderbox.

"Crash priority! Clear channels to Generalissimo Chavez!"

At the door of the room in the tourist hotel, Sid Jakes turned to the three security officers who were escorting him and Li Chang.

He said, "I suggest that you remain here, until we have dealt with him. This is the most dangerous man in all United Planets."

Desmond said, "Our orders are to cooperate with you to the utmost. It has been accepted that El Primero's life is at stake."

Sid Jakes knocked and, without waiting for an answer, flung open the door. Li Chang entered first. They didn't want to startle the other and were aware that Sam Goodboy knew her the best.

The drab little man was in the process of seating himself before the room's Tri-Di stage. He looked up in surprise. He said, "Why, Supervisor Chu!" He blinked and his eyes went in turn to Sid Jakes. Sid closed the door behind him, blocking the view of the security men beyond.

Li Chang blurted, "Sam! Everything has been changed! You must not kill El Primero."

He looked at her blankly, and then at Sid Jakes. He was aghast. He said in distress, "But . . . but I have already killed him."

Li Chang collapsed into a chair. "Oh, no."

For the briefest of moments, Sid Jakes closed his eyes in pain. Ronald Bronston had not only been his best operative, but he was also a close personal friend. But then he brought himself, as he must, back to the immediate reality.

He snapped, "The fat's in the fire now. We've got to rescue what we can. We've got to get out of here someway; and back to the *Gremlin.* Ronny's gone, and there's nothing we can do about it. It was nobody's deliberate fault."

Sam Goodboy was looking back and forth between them, his face in dismay, ineffectual as never before. He said plaintively, "I . . . I don't understand. I . . . I followed orders exactly. I've never done this sort of thing before. On my home planet, I used to work occasionally for the police. Some escaped mad killer or something like that."

Sid's eyes had been darting about the room, looking for another exit. There was none. He went to the window and stared down. Six stories of smooth wall.

"You killed the wrong man," he bit out.

"But . . . I never kill the wrong man."

"One of our agents, Ronny Bronston, somehow infiltrated the palace and took Ortega's place."

"Oh, *that,*" Sam Goodboy said, in relief.

"Oh, *that?*" Li Chang said. "You're talking about——"

165

"Oh, I didn't kill *Ronny*," Sam explained seriously. "My orders were to kill El Primero, not somebody disguised as him. And just in time, too. He had managed to escape from where Ronny had him locked up and was about to reorganize his men to recapture the palace. Oh, he's very dead."

The Tri-Di stage lit up, and there, standing alone, simply garbed in a Dorian enlisted man's uniform, without decoration, stood a strong-faced, domineering personality.

The three dimensioned figure, lifelike, save in size, stared out at them for a moment, then spoke. "Citizens of Doria!" he began. "I have a most important message."

"There's Ronny now," Sam Goodboy said in satisfaction.

Sid Jakes stared at him, as did Li Chang, then both turned and stared at the Tri-Di figure, now fully launched into its epic speech.

"How did you know?" Sid demanded.

The little man squirmed. "I don't know," he said in apology. "It all just kind of comes to me. But I never make mistakes. I never kill the wrong person. That would be awful."

XIX

"Shot!" the colonel rasped. "El Caudillo shot!"

Raul Dobarganes said, unbelievingly. "Dead. Shot dead. The parade in Almeria. The parade in honor of the glorious matadors who have fallen in the arena. The assassins were stationed all along the route of the parade. There must have been at least five of them in all. The fourth gunman got him. El Caudillo is dead."

Horsten winced. He muttered, "I didn't expect them to be so susceptible, when I told them that story."

Helen looked at him, speculatively. "Are you sure?"

"I don't know," he said defensively. "I suppose it doesn't make much difference now."

The colonel had sped from the room, roaring orders right and left.

Pierre Lorans found the courage to laugh. "Well, at least it will probably give us a respite for an hour or so."

Martha said, "More than that." Her eyes seemed to go empty and she recited, "*Falange Legal Code, Article Three, Section Three. During the National Fiesta Brava and until the new Caudillo is confirmed, there are no criminals on the planet Falange. Each resident must be free to compete as a torero if such is his desire . . .*"

Horsten looked his astonishment. "You mean they open the prisons?"

"Evidently. It must be a madhouse."

Helen growled. "Let's get out of here and back to the hotel. Evidently, there's nothing to stop us." She looked over at the shaken Raul Dobarganes. "Is there, cutey?"

He had been taking in their conversation, dazedly. In actuality, the last National Fiesta Brava had been held while he was still so young that few of the details remained with him. All he could recall was the great excitement. Now, he was almost as confused as the Section G operatives by the sudden change in the situation.

However, he knew the law. He shook his head. "No. There is nothing to stop you. There are no criminals on Falange. But as soon as the new Caudillo has been selected, you will again be apprehended and your trial will take place."

Helen winked at him and said to the others, "Let's go folks."

They stood on the balcony of the Lorans suite at the Posada San Francisco and looked glumly down at the merrymaking crowds.

"Look at those costumes," Martha said. "You would have thought that it would take weeks to make some of them."

Horsten grunted and said, "They were out on the streets within half an hour of the flashing of the news of El Caudillo's death."

Bartolome Guerro was with them, his expression sour. "For some of them, it is the one real excitement of their lives. The world turned upside down. The peon is free to leave the *finca* and journey into town for the local *corridas*. If he has the wherewithal, he can even make the trip here to Nuevo Madrid for the finals. The poorest laborer, in fiesta costume, rubs shoulders with the wealthiest *hidalgo,* may steal a kiss, if he's handsome enough, from a titled lady."

Helen said, staring down at the mobs of dancing, running, laughing, drinking, milling Falangists, "And this is going on all over the planet?"

Guerro nodded. "Everywhere. There are few towns so small as not to have a bullring. It is the Falange equivalent of the Roman circus, and serves the same purpose. So long as the people are completely caught up in the fiesta brava, they have little time to realize the inadequacies of the life they lead. And this is the fiesta of all fiestas. The National Fiesta Brava, seldom witnessed more than once or twice in a single man's lifetime."

Dorn Horsten said, "And the elimination fights are taking place throughout the planet?"

"That is correct. Local toreros fight in their local arenas. The best is then sent to the county seat, where he competes with those others who have survived the local *corridas.* From there, he goes to the nearest large city, and eventually here to Nuevo Madrid for the finals. Thousands of *corridas* are being held all over Falange at this very moment."

Pierre Lorans said, "How is it decided who wins? It would seem to me that it could be rigged by the judges."

The Falangist shook his head. "No, that is not where the rigging comes in. It is the crowd that decides, by popular acclaim, and no judge would dare go against it. If a torero fights well, he is awarded an ear, if he fights superlatively he will get two ears. If he triumphs, he gets two ears and a tail. On the rarest of occasions, he is awarded a hoof on top of all the rest."

169

Horsten was looking at him questioningly. "Where does the rigging come in?" he said. "I've wondered about this before. How can the ruling class take the chance that some peon or other lower case member, might win and upset the applecart?"

The other grunted deprecation. "Theoretically, it's all fair. However, the sons of the elite *finca* owners begin playing with fighting bulls when they are two or three years old—and the bulls two or three days old. By the time they are ten, instructed by the most competent veterans of the arena, they fight calves. By the time they're twelve, they are fighting small bulls at *tientas,* the testing of the young bulls. At about the same time they are allowed to kill steers at the ranch slaughterhouse, literally by the hundreds, learning every trick of the game. Ah, believe me, my friends, by the time our young *hidalgo* is sixteen he knows just about everything there is to know about the *Bos taurus ibericus* and the fiestas brava."

The Section G agents had been interested. Lorans said, "Any other way they have of getting an advantage?"

Guerro made his very Iberian shrug. "Well, the matador's *caudrillas*; his assistants, *picadors, banderilleros,* and peons. They have a double purpose, one, to come to his rescue when he's in trouble, and, two, to make him look good in the ring. If a man can afford the most expensive *caudrilla* that it is possible to hire, then he has a big advantage. On the face of it, one of Falange's ruling elite can so afford, and some youngster up from the slums hasn't got a chance of acquiring top assistants."

Helen said suddenly, "What's the latest from our boy? How's Jose Hoyos doing?"

Guerro pulled a great gust of air down into his lungs. "He is doing . . . adequately. The crowds call him Joseito and he is still Numero Tres. Number One and Number Two, *hildagos* named Perico and Calitos by their fans, have been shifting back and forth as favorites, but Joseito has consistently remained third in popularity. None of these top three have had a serious goring yet, they've all been lucky."

"Third place, eh? How about his, what did you call it, his assistants?" Horsten said.

"His *caudrilla*? Top men. All members of the Lorca Party, all professional toreros. They're nearly as good as those of either Numero Uno or Numero Dos." There was a shine in the gaunt man's eyes. "For once, we have possibly an even chance. For once, one of ours will at least participate in the finals. If he could only make it! El Caudillo! One of our party!"

The sounds of the mobs dancing in the streets wafted up to them. It was an insane asylum down below.

Helen said, "Is it going to be possible for us to watch the final fights?"

"Why not?" the Falangist revolutionary told her. "It is simply a matter of being willing to pay enough for tickets. People have been known to sell their homes, beggar themselves, to buy a ticket for the final *corrida*. The arena sits but fifty thousand and all Falange would like to attend. However, I imagine that with United Planets resources behind you. . . ."

Martha said grimly, "We have to be there to cheer on Joseito. If he wins, we've got it made, mission accomplished and everything. If he loses, Colonel Segura will have us back in the Alcazar before we can blink."

Guerro looked at her, frowning. "Couldn't you make a run for it now?" He looked around at the others.

Horsten grunted. "Run to where?" he said. "They certainly aren't going to let us get aboard a spaceship, even if there was one available, and there isn't. Please make arrangements for us to attend the fight. Price is no object."

Whatever the moral implications of the fiesta brava, either in the old days in Spain and Mexico, or on the planet Falange, a colorful spectacle beyond compare it most certainly is.

Fifty thousand persons packed the seats, and another ten or more stood in the rear and in the aisles. All were dressed in their most colorful best. All brimmed with excitement. The bands blared out the *Diana*, song of the bullfight, hawkers took beer, soft drinks, nuts and other edibles through the crowd, friends screamed greetings at each other over the heads of intervening hundreds. Fans and handkerchiefs flutered. Masculine *aficionados* cheered each time a youthful senorita found it necessary to hike full skirts a fraction in order to climb over stone seats, seeking her own reserved space.

The Section G operatives, still accompanied by Bartolome Guerro, had superlative seats right on the *barrera*, immediately above the *callejon*, the passage which circles the arena proper and behind which the toreros, not immediately in action, shelter themselves during the *corrida*. It would have been impossible to have been any closer to the action without joining it. Immediately to their left was the gate of the bull, which led back from the arena to the *toril*, the bull's enclosure.

None of them, save Guerro, had ever seen a *corrida*, with the exception of portions in a Tri-Di historical tape on Earth or one of the other advanced planets.

The Falangist revolutionist explained procedure to

them as the afternoon wore on. There were three matadors, Carlitos, Perico and Joseito, who had wound up in
the finals, Numeros Uno, Dos and Tres. Joseito, the Lorca
Party champion, was Numero Tres, as he had been consistently through the preliminary fights.

Carlitos, a tall, beautifully graceful man of possibly
thirty, was to have the first bull. Scion of one of the
planet's wealthiest rancher families, he had for years
been one of Falange's most popular matadors and was
by far and gone the favorite of the crowd.

Perico, a smaller, dark-complexioned man, was not
nearly the physical specimen his opponent was, but evidently, from what Guerro said, was noted for the impossible chances he took, the *desplantes* he indulged in so
arrogantly, the *adornos*. He was famous for taking the
tip of a dominated bull's horn in his mouth, to the horror
of the crowd. A sudden flip upward of the horn and his
brain would have been pierced. He too was of one of the
very best families.

The preliminary parade, each matador followed by his
caudrilla, brought the audience cheering to its feet, each
shouting the name of his champion.

To the swinging strains of *La Golondrina,* that song of
the torero come down through the centuries, they
marched to the judge's stand and made their salute, in
dim, dim memory of the gladiators who once stood and
shouted up to their emperor, "*We who are about to
die. . . .*"

The *caudrillas* dispersed, most to take their places in
the *callejon* until it was time for their own performance.
The peons of Carlitos remained in the ring, spaced
around, waiting for the first bull.

He came exploding into the ring, half a ton and more

173

of deliberately bred trouble. Deliberately bred for thousands of years to meet death in the afternoon, in the arena.

Carlitos stood alone in the ring center, his cape gently in hands. The bull spotted him and again exploded.

Helen sucked in her breath.

Guerro explained. "He is noted for his *Veronicas*. Some say he is the greatest master of the *Veronica* since the legendary Manolete of Spain. It is the most graceful of cape passes and the basic of them all."

Carlitos made no preliminary passes to gauge the bull's mettle. The first pass was taken inches from the bull's horns and the second and the third. The crowd screamed its *oles*.

Guerro wiped his brow with a handkerchief. "He is unbelievable," he said. "Joseito could never present such *Veronicas*."

Helen looked at him. "So far we're losing, eh?"

"Nobody on Falange could perform such *Veronicas*, save Carlitos," Guerro said unhappily.

Lorans growled, "Why does that confounded bull charge so straight? The slightest deviation and our torero would have a horn in the guts."

"It is a perfect bull, Senor Lorans," Guerro admitted. "They are bred to run straight. When a matador has such a bull, he is assured of a triumph. Carlitos is fortunate. His bull is perfect. We can only pray that Joseito has similar fortune."

The matador passed the animal eight times before finally bringing it to a frustrated standstill and stalking arrogantly away, not bothering to look over his shoulder to see if the animal was making one last charge.

The fight proceeded through the quarter of the *picadors,* through the quarter of the *banderillas.*

Guerro wiped his forehead again. "Perfect," he said. "Everything perfect. It is possibly the most superlative *corrida* I have ever seen."

"We're losing, eh?" Helen said lowly. "And our boy hasn't even been to bat yet."

For the moment, the bull stood immediately below them, breathing deeply from his exertions, waiting while Carlitos selected his sword and *muleta.* Waiting while Carlitos dedicated the animal to the three judges of the National Fiesta Brava finals. The matador wound it up by tossing his hat back over his shoulder into the stands and advancing toward the animal.

Pierre Lorans pursed plump lips. "Those are strange looking horns," he muttered.

Guerro looked at him. "Beef animals no longer have such horns, it is true. Bue these are specially bred fighting bulls, and the wide horn spread and length are necessary for a proper *corrida."*

"It is not that," Lorans grumbled. "As an apprentice at the Cordon Bleu school, I had to become a butcher. One cannot cook if one does not know what he cooks. Each Cordon Bleu chef is a butcher as well as many other things. And I say. . . ."

He lost the attention of his listeners as Carlitos went into his *faena,* the final series of passes that culminate in the moment of truth, the bull's death.

The kill was perfect, the bull dropped as though he had been poleaxed. Carlitos paraded the ring, the crowd cheering. He and his assistants held up his award, two ears, the tail and a hoof.

175

"The highest possible award," Guerro told them, wiping his mouth in despair with his handkerchief.

Perico had the next bull, a *cardeno*, Guerro explained, an animal with a mixed black and white coat.

The dark matador lived up to his reputation for foolhardy chances by beginning the fight on his knees, his cape spread out before him, his arms spread wide, as though in supplication to the bull. Immediately upon entering the ring, it spotted him and banged in his direction.

Helen closed her eyes; seemingly, there was no chance of the bullfighter avoiding destruction. At the last split second, the matador grabbed up the cape and fluttered it to one side, and the animal exploded past. The crowd screamed itself hoarse.

Perico was awarded two ears and a tail. Not quite as much as Carlitos had taken, but each had one more bull to fight.

It was the turn of Joseito. Elements in the crowd yelled, "Lorca! Lorca!"

Dorn Horsten looked at Guerro, who shook his head. "They take their chances, but the rumor has been deliberately spread. They know Joseito is the champion of the Lorca Party and what it means if he is proclaimed El Caudillo."

Martha was looking about the stands, in this short period between fights. She said to Helen, "I wonder where your boyfriend is, the brain surgeon."

Something came to Helen out of the blue.

She muttered, "Brain surgeon . . . electronics technician." She turned to Martha quickly. "When Colonel Segura and his stooge were interrogating us about the ash in the fireplace. What was it he said about Ferd Zogbaum?"

Martha scowled momentarily, but then her eyes went empty and she recited, "The assistant said, *'Probably the technician for the* corridas, *Senor Colonel. He arrived on the same spaceship, you'll recall. Senor Zogbaum."*

"Technician for the *corridas*," Helen snarled. "What kind of technician? A brain surgeon!"

Lorans hadn't been listening. He was scowling at the new bull, Joseito's bull, that had just come dashing into the ring in a great swirl of dust. "As a butcher," he muttered, "they are the strangest horns I have ever seen. They are not——"

"They're not horns, they're radio antennas!" Helen snapped suddenly. "Come on, Pete. Those animals are being controlled, the deck's stacked! Come on Dorn! Martha, you stay here and keep your eyes open." With no more than that, the diminutive acrobat vaulted over the *barrera* wall into the *callejon* below, the two masculine Section G operatives only split seconds behind her.

Startled ring attendants reacted too slowly to halt the progress of the unlikely looking three. The little girl, the hulking giant wearing pince-nez glasses, and the puffing, heavy-set, servant type bringing up the rear. They ducked, dodged and elbowed their way around the wooden shelter.

Horsten, who had immediately accepted her words, as had Lorans, called, "What are we looking for?"

"It must be somewhere right on the ring, where the fight can be watched," she called back. "Some kind of a control room. "What's *that*?" She skidded to a halt.

177

"One of the infirmaries," Lorans puffed. "Guerro pointed it out. For emergency gorings. Behind this one is the chapel of the United Temple."

"Those opaque windows," Helen snapped. "Polarized glass. Infirmary my foot! Come on!"

Two *Guardia Civil* attempted to stop them, and nearly had their chests caved in by the sweeping arm of Dorn Horsten. The door was heavy, closed and evidently barred from within.

"Dorn!" Helen said.

His heavy shoulder crashed into the wooden barrier.

Behind them, the crowd had gone hysterical, shouting over and over, *"Ole, ole, ole!!!"* at whatever it was Joseito was doing with his bull.

The door caved in, even as Guardia Civil and *Policia Secreta* plainclothesmen approached at the double, guns drawn.

Inside, Ferd Zogbaum looked up and blinked. He was seated at a control board, a headset over his ears, a dozen dials and an equal number of switches before him.

At one of the windows, binoculars to eyes, stood a uniformed comandante of the *Policia Secreta*. Even as the trio burst into the room unceremoniously, he was saying, "The right horn, a quick toss."

Ferd Zogbuam's small hands were dancing over the control switches.

Helen snapped, "Pete!"

The ballbearings came so fast that seemingly there were a score of them in the air at once. Tubes crashed, dials shattered, Ferd Zogbaum's headset was torn magically from his head. In split seconds the room was an electronic shambles.

178

Helen stood there, hand on hips and stared at Zogbaum. "Aren't you ashamed of yourself?"

He blinked, then blurted, "To tell the truth, yes. But there was nothing I could do. I wasn't clear on what this job was when they hired me, but the pay was fantastic. The old technician had died. He was from Earth, too. They hire you for life; they don't have men here capable of operating this equipment, and they use it at every major fight in this arena."

Horsten was staring around the room. He looked out the oneway window, after brushing the startled *Policia Secreta* comandante to one side.

"I knew it!" he growled. "It had to come to something like this. The big *corrida* rigged. Electrodes attached to the brain of the animal. Radio impulses from this control booth, causing the bull to dash straight ahead, without veering, or to toss to right or left, as electronically ordered."

Martha and Guerro entered from behind them. Her face was gray. "Whatever you found, it's too late," she said.

"What do you mean!" Helen said.

"Joseito," Guerro said emptily. "He has taken a *cornada.*"

"A what?"

"He has been gored. Seriously. He is out of the running."

"Then . . . then we can't possibly win."

A new voice came from the door. It was Colonel Segura, military revolver in hand. "No," he said. "You can't possibly win, you of the Lorca Party, you of Section G. You have lost. Within fifteen minutes, the fight will

179

be decided. Either Carlitos or Perico will be declared the new El Caudillo and all of you will be brought to trial on subversion charges."

Helen glared at him. "Not quite yet, you funker. Come on Dorn, Pete, Martha. To the judge's stand!"

"Why?" Lorans said, hope gone from his voice.

"Because I just remembered something Martha recited to us from the Tauromachy Code."

Dorn led the way again, pushing through police and ring attendants, finding an exit that led upward into the *tenidos,* the stands. They pushed and wedged themselves through packed aisles on the way to the box of the presiding judges of the National Fiesta Brava.

A bevy of *Guardia Civil* was the ultimate obstacle to their getting through. Dorn Horsten brushed them aside. Helen, chubby hands on hips, confronted the three aged judges.

She said shrilly, "I declare myself a contestant and demand the right to fight!"

There was only astonishment in the faces of the three Falangists. Colonel Segura had scurried to the box. He bent over the judges and whispered to them.

One went to the trouble of saying, "Please, Senorita, this is a most serious event. It is no time for jest. Joseito has been eliminated from the corridas, but two bulls remain to be fought."

"I'm not joking," Helen bit out. "I demand the right to participate."

"Hey," Horsten said. "What about me?"

"You lumbering ox," Helen growled under her breath. "Support me. I've got an idea." She turned back to the judges. "We quote from the Tauromachy Code. Martha!

180

That section on discovery of fraud in the National Fiesta Brava."

Martha's eyes went lackluster. She said, "*Tauromachy Code. Article Eight, Section Two. If a participant can prove fraud in the National Fiesta Brava, he may demand to enter the eliminations on the level the fraud was revealed, even though he already had been eliminated.*"

"That's it!" Helen said. "I declare myself a participant. The evidence of fraud is there to be seen in the supposed infirmary. The bulls were being directed by radio, through electrodes embedded in their skulls."

The judges stared at each other. Colonel Segura bowed over them again and whispered.

One said snappishly, "You're a woman!"

"Martha!"

"There is nothing in the Tauromachy Code preventing a woman from fighting in the National Fiesta Brava. Women matadors are not unknown. I quote from the Juno 335, of the year of Falange, issue of *El Toro Magazine. The Senorita Octoviana Gonzales participated as a* rejoneadore *and cut two ears at the Plaza de Toros in the town of Nuevo Murcia today. The occasion was . . .*"

One of the judges leaned forward angrily. A deep hush had fallen over the arena, as though the sixty-thousand spectators were attempting to hear what was being said —an impossibility to all except those in the immediate vicinity.

The judge said, "Admittedly, women have, on rare occasion, and usually on their own fincas, very informally, participated in *corridas*——"

"There is nothing in Falange law preventing a woman from participating in the National Fiesta Brava," Martha said stubbornly.

181

SECTION G: UNITED PLANETS

"You are a criminal alien!" the third of the judges barked, breaking his silence for the first time.

Helen said strongly, "There is nothing in Falange law to prevent a criminal from participating, nor need I be a citizen. I am a temporary resident of Falange and subject to its laws, and eligible to participate."

"Why, you're not even a grown woman," the first judge bleated indignantly.

Helen flushed her anger. "I am a normal woman and citizen of the planet Lilliput where my size is not inordinary," she flared. "But now I am a resident of Falange and demand my right to participate in the eliminations."

The third judge turned sly. "Very well, Senorita. However, you must realize that there are certain requirements, instituted to eliminate some of the early would-be contestants so as to speed up the National Fiesta Brava. Our national spectacle is highly stylized. Each participant must fight in a given school. What school do you choose?"

"School?" Helen said blankly.

The judge was triumphant. "We do not let the fiesta brava become a comic farce. Do you fight *La Ronda* style, *Seville* style, or *Madrid* style? If you choose one, then you must stick to that school of bullfighting."

Helen's eyes darted around desperately. Her face pleaded at Dorn Horsten, then Pierre Lorans. Both shook their heads, blankly.

The judge whinnied amusement. "Come. What school do you fight in, Senorita?"

She snapped, "I fight Cretan style!"

They gaped at her.

Helen said, "Surely anybody claiming a knowledge of the history of bull fighting realizes that the earliest and most venerable style of all is that once practiced at the

182

Minoan palace of Knossus on the island of Crete, two thousand and more years before the fiesta brava was ever dreamed of in Spain."

Deep rumblings were going through the crowd, even as Martha and Helen improvised a Cretan kilt for her costume. Rumors were evidently flying, and Guerro's underground adherents of the Lorca Party were doing their best to make hay. The National Fiesta Brava was rigged!

Dorn Horsten was to act as her *sobresaliente,* her sole assistant in the ring. There was no time to costume him. He peeled down to trousers and shirt, which he left open at the neck, and kicked off his shoes, the better to operate in the sand of the arena.

Helen dashed into the ring, followed by the lumbering Dorn Horsten, even as the *Bos taurus ibericus* came charging in from the other side.

Diminutive she still was, fearfully so in view of the size of the rampaging animal, but child she was not longer. That was obvious to all.

She sped toward the beast. He spotted her, changed slightly his line of charge and with the speed of a locomotive, came storming down.

The shouts from the crowd were of horror.

The bull was scant feet away, animal and tiny human still heading full toward each other. It lowered its head to toss, and for a moment they seemed to blend.

Small chubby hands went out, seized horn tips. The bull tossed, she spun over his head in a somersault, landed on her feet on his back, facing toward his hind quarters. She somersaulted again, off his back and to the sands beyond. Dorn Horsten caught and steadied her.

The mob in the arena stands screamed in disbelief.

183

The bull was heading back. The performance was repeated. And again and again.

At long last, the bewildered animal was exhausted, run to a standstill. It stood there, head lowered, tongue hanging out, breathing deeply, confused, dominated.

The stands were a madhouse. The stands were screaming confusion. The stands were bedlam.

There was nothing more that could be done with the exhausted animal. Helen began a tour of the ring, in somewhat the fasion the matadors had done earlier when they had received their ears, tails and hoofs of their fallen victims.

But she did it with a difference. She toured the ring like a pinwheel, a top, a bouncing, spinning, cartwheeling demonstration of acrobatics such as had never been seen on the staid old planet of Falange before.

And behind her, running as the assistants of the matadors had run behind their principales earlier, came the lumbering Doctor Dorn Horsten, pince-nez glasses still firmly on his nose.

Only with a difference. He did not carry the awarded ears, tail and hoofs as had the assistants of Carlitos and Percio.

Slung over his shoulders he carried the bewildered bull.

The stands were now screaming laughter.

AFTERWARD

They were rehashing the details in the suite of the
Posada San Francisco. The Section G operatives were present, Bartolome Guerro, a highly bandaged Jose Hoyos
and a dozen others from the upper echelons of the once
underground organization, the Lorca Party.

Dorn Horsten was summing it up. "No government
can stand in the face of ridicule. No government can
stand without dignity. Any government that becomes far-
cical, falls. Nero, with all his power, with all the traditions
of the deified Caesars behind him, fell when he allowed
himself to appear the clown."

Guerro was nodding agreement. "How quickly the institution of El Caudillo became a laughingstock when a
tiny girl took over the title, after first revealing the games
were dishonest and then making a mockery of the national spectacle."

Helen entered the room, dressed now not as an eight-
year-old but in the latest Falange style, including flamenco style high heels and a touch of lipstick.

Horsten looked at her, somewhat taken aback. "Where
are you going?"

She said snappishly, "What business is it of yours, you
overgrown lummox? But if you must know, I have a date

with Ferd Zogbaum. First, I'm going to give the cloddy a knockdown and dragout dressing-down. Then I'm going to relent. After all, he is the nearest thing to a man my size for a couple of hundred light years." She added, a devilish glint in her eyes, "And I suspect he had new opinions about little Helen since seeing me in that Cretan costume."